Van

P9-CLW-804

A PHANTOM DEATH

A PHANTOM DEATH

•

Annette Mahon

AVALON BOOKS
NEW YORK

Mah

© Copyright 2000 by Annette Mahon
Library of Congress Catalog Card Number: 00-100783
ISBN 0-8034-9429-7
All rights reserved.
All the characters in this book are fictitious,
and any resemblance to actual persons,
living or dead, is purely coincidental.
Published by Thomas Bouregy & Co., Inc.
160 Madison Avenue, New York, NY 10016

PRINTED IN THE UNITED STATES OF AMERICA
ON ACID-FREE PAPER
BY HADDON CRAFTSMEN, BLOOMSBURG, PENNSYLVANIA

7/00
TB+CO

For my wonderful, supportive family,
who continue to encourage me in my writing.

Prologue

It was a glorious night, crisp and clear, with millions of tiny shards of light sparkling in the deep black of the desert sky. A crescent moon shone, providing a soft silver glow to the landscape.

Jon drove down an unpaved access road that led to what he hoped would soon be his property. He was avoiding the main street and driving with his headlights off, not wanting to chance disturbing his soon-to-be neighbors at this indecent hour of the morning. But the urge to show off this bit of the American dream was too strong to ignore.

He steered the Oldsmobile Bravada toward the end of the trail, stopping where it narrowed. From here it became nothing more than a dusty horse trail. He put on the emergency brake. The terrain was hilly, the car new, and although it could easily have climbed to the top of the mountain, he preferred to keep to more amicable ground. After all, the car too was part of the American dream.

They were in the foothills now, the dark bulk of the mountains towering above them. The click of the car door sounded unnaturally loud in the still darkness, disturbing a coyote who howled into the night. Little scuttling noises heralded the presence of smaller creatures scurrying away from this strange, intrusive presence. The night, after all, was supposed to be theirs.

Jon breathed in deeply. He wanted to burst into song, to celebrate the fact that at the age of thirty-two he was finally making enough in his profession to own a good vehicle and contemplate buying this property. Enough to build a dream home.

"Isn't this wonderful?" He waved his arms to encompass the whole area. "Look at the stars. You don't see those in L.A. And this air is so fresh and invigorating." He took in another deep breath, enjoying the earthy scents of soil and horses and the faint perfume of citrus trees blooming somewhere nearby.

He waved his arm, anxious to show off his little bit of paradise and to reminisce about his youth. "Come on. It's over this way."

His companion, however, seemed reluctant to move too far away from the car. "Yeah. Nice. But it's awfully dark. Maybe I'll see it another time."

Jon laughed, the sound bouncing off the mountain and back toward them. "Oh, come on. It's safe. Just watch out for scorpions. There shouldn't be any snakes at night, but now is when the scorpions come out. We could see them if we had a black light—it makes them glow in the dark." He walked farther into the desert as he talked, striding confidently through the scrubby undergrowth.

"Scorpions? Snakes?" The voice trailing after him turned shrill. "How far are we from civilization? Maybe I could wait."

Another laugh. "Where's your sense of adventure? Besides, we're far from anywhere right now. And you haven't seen it yet."

"It's too dark." The disembodied voice was almost a whine. "How can you see anything?"

Jon refused to let such petty complaints dilute his own enjoyment. He was exuberant. This feeling he had tonight was sheer joy because soon he would be back to his hometown. This would be the happiest time of his life.

"I can see just fine." Jon laughed with delight. "I'm the Phantom. I wander through the night, a creature of the darkness." He hummed a snatch of song as he strolled through the desert.

His footsteps sounded loud on the hard-packed soil, crunching on natural debris as he moved through the land he'd just seen the other day—the first time in twenty years. The desert floor was littered with stones and skeletal bits of cacti. Yet it must have been a wet winter, as clumps of wildflowers almost past their peak were everywhere. Although the bit of moonlight made it bright enough to see his way clearly, Jon wished for daylight, when the blooms would be open wide to the sun, their colorful faces brightening the desert landscape. Now they nodded silently at his passing, closed tight against the night's cold.

"This is the land I'm going to buy," he shouted to his unseen companion. This was what he'd wanted to see again, what he wanted to show off. "I'm going to build a house. A marvelous house. I can just see it. Four bedrooms. Big rooms and high ceilings. Lots of windows. A swimming pool. Guest house. Tennis courts." He shouted out each feature as it occurred to him, picturing the mansion he'd build and the wonderful views it would command. "Oh, it'll be glorious!"

Jon stopped to admire a saguaro, its dark shadow clearly outlined against the moonlit sky. Huge and statue-like it must have stood in this spot for many hundreds of years. As a child, a favorite pastime of his had been sitting near the towering cacti, dreaming of a time when Wyatt Earp or Geronimo or some other equally colorful Arizona figure might have stood in the same spot, staring at the same cactus.

He paused for a moment, his eyes glued to the strange shape of the saguaro. The placement of the arms was unusual. Jon had a sudden cartoon-like vision of the saguaro standing in the middle of an intersection, a crazy four-armed policeman, directing traffic consisting of rabbits and hares, gila monsters and coyotes. The absurd vision made him stop suddenly, and in the stillness he heard footsteps behind him.

He must have played here as a child. He and his friends rode all over this area, even playing a game much like the cloud game where they attributed pictures to the cacti. "That one looks like the bad guy with his arms in the air." "No, like an acrobat balancing on one hand."

The crunch of a footfall came again. Jon shook his head to clear it of fanciful thoughts. "There you are. Took you long enough. What do you think of it?"

Jon turned, ready to greet his companion, a comment about fearing the dark, the desert, and its creatures ready on his lips. He was unprepared for the ducking shadow, the quick sprint, the sudden lunge.

With the sharp pain and the flooding darkness of death came one quick, final thought. What had he done to deserve this?

Chapter One

Maggie Browne and the other women of the St. Rose Quilting Bee moved around their workroom off the church courtyard, putting a quilt into the frame. On Friday, they had finished the quilting on an appliqué iris top and Anna Howard had taken it home to apply the binding. It now rested in their closet, carefully wrapped in a white cotton sheet, and a new top was being readied for quilting.

The St. Rose Quilting Bee was part of the St. Rose Seniors' Guild, a large group mostly of retired individuals who met at St. Rose Catholic Church every morning for companionship and crafts. St. Rose was an older parish in the southern part of Scottsdale, Arizona. Father Bob O'Connell had decided some years ago to offer activities for the increasing numbers of newly retired parishioners. And so the Seniors' Guild was born.

Every October, the Guild staged their Halloween Craft Fair, which had become a popular neighborhood event. From the beginning, the Craft Fair had included a quilt raffle. As the Seniors' Guild grew and the Quilting Bee added members, the women were able to complete more and more quilts. Then a member of the Guild, who had been in public relations work and advertising, had seen the potential for success in the exquisite work produced by the Bee. Five years ago, he had organized an auction, with six beautifully pierced and appliquéd quilts up for sale. Last year the women had produced twelve quilts and bidders had come from five states and one Canadian province. And they still produced one quilt for the raffle—the last quilt they made, just before the grand event. It was always an appliquéd rose pattern, always exquisite.

This morning the women were putting a Grandmother's Fan top into the quilting frame, and stitching on it would begin before they left for the day. As they stretched the backing fabric across the frame, Clare Patterson rushed into the room.

"Sorry I'm late." She dropped her purse on the closet shelf reserved for that purpose and turned, her agitated manner causing the others to pause in their work.

"You won't believe what I just heard on the car radio." Her eyes, clouded with concern, fastened on Maggie. "Jonathan Hunter's been murdered."

Maggie stopped pinning, the stretched fabric loosening in her hands as she raised questioning eyes to Clare. "I beg your pardon?"

"I just heard it on the car radio," Clare repeated. "His body was found by a woman walking her dog. Out north, in the mountains."

Maggie's grip loosened even more, causing Victoria Farrington beside her to take the fabric from her hands in order to maintain the proper tension.

"Murdered? What in the world—" The usually unflappable Maggie turned pale beneath her sun-browned cheeks. Lean and athletic even in her retirement years, her skin brown and leathery from years of exposure to the hot desert sun, Maggie still looked like the rancher's wife she'd been for much of her life.

"Murdered," Maggie repeated.

Clare moved to Victoria's side, taking Maggie's place. "Some poor woman out at sunrise, walking her dog, they said. Imagine." Clare shivered, her shoulders pulling in close to her body. "It makes me think I should just let poor Grayson get his exercise in the yard every morning." Clare shook her head at the thought of encountering a body on her morning walk with her beloved miniature schnauzer.

"But then you'd miss your exercise as well," Louise Lombard cautioned her. "And didn't your doctor tell you you need those walks as much as Grayson does?"

Clare nodded.

"And you don't walk at sunrise anyway," Anna reminded her. "You always say that you don't go until you get Gerald his breakfast and he heads off to the golf course. I don't know why there would be a body on your street, Clare, but if there was, someone else would find it first."

Clare brightened at that, agreeing that many other people took their dogs out before she did, or at approximately the same time.

"Things are getting so bad these days, even your street might not be safe," Edie Dulinski intoned gloomily.

The others quickly changed the subject. Edie liked nothing more than harping on disaster, and one of her favorite topics was the increasing crime rate.

But within minutes, Clare mentioned again where the body had been found. "It was out in the mountains, out where you used to live, Maggie."

If possible, Maggie turned even paler. Worried, Victoria left the quilt to the others and led Maggie to a chair.

"I'm fine," Maggie insisted, hating to be fussed over but still in a state of shock. *Out near Hal's.* The thought of a murder so close to her son's home made her heart rate increase. Maggie's oldest son now lived on the ranch she and her husband had worked on all their happy years together. And he had two young boys of his own. Thank goodness they were out of town. But still, it was too close.

Maggie had to pull her mind away from thoughts of her family when she realized Louise was addressing her.

"He must have lived out there when you knew him," Louise was saying. Louise had the same practical outlook that Maggie usually showed; it was a measure of Maggie's shock that she was so distracted now.

"Yes. Of course." Maggie, still pale but recovering, pulled herself to her feet. "He and his family lived not too far from the ranch."

Maggie moved forward to resume helping with the quilt. She had to *do* something, or she would break down completely just sitting there thinking—thinking of a young man her son Michael's age, murdered.

The women had finished pinning the stretched backing fabric and were spreading out the polyester batting. Maggie resumed her place on one side of the quilt frame, helping smooth the batting without stretching it too thin. The entire process of layering the quilt was second nature to them, however, and the conversation continued.

"The Hunters had a small place," Maggie went on. "Like I said, not too far from us. Jon was always at our house playing with the boys. He was a lovely child, so cute with his dark curly hair. And the sweetest manners. Even then, he liked to sing. Because of the horses, they always played cowboys or rodeo and my boys teased him about becoming a singing cowboy."

"So what do you suppose happened?" Clare used a wooden yardstick to smooth the batting at the center of the frame, moving the smooth wand across the fluffy white sheet until it lay unwrinkled and flat.

"He probably got in the way of some gang." Edie always had a theory, usually having to do with street gangs or transients.

Anna's eyes widened. "In the mountains?" The area around the Brownes' ranch was being aggressively developed, and exclusive subdivisions were the rule. But in the immediate neighborhood of the Brownes, small ranches still sat amid lovely natural desert, the mountains rising up beyond it.

"I think gang violence usually takes place in the city," Louise remarked. "And usually involves guns. Was he shot?"

The women stopped working as they all looked to Clare for the answer. But all she could do was look flustered and shake her head. "They didn't say."

Clare wasn't the only one who was disappointed by this answer.

"Maybe he was visiting his old home," Victoria suggested.

As she picked up the quilt top and began to spread it over the other two layers, Maggie nodded thoughtfully. "That's the most promising suggestion so far," she admitted. "But I do wish we had a better idea of what happened. It's too close to Hal's place for me to feel comfortable."

"Isn't he out of town?" Anna asked.

"Yes. They get back on Thursday."

"We'll have to listen to the evening news," Louise decided. "And check the paper tomorrow morning."

As they busily inserted pins into the quilt's layers, they discussed which of the television news stations they preferred. The pros and cons of the various news anchors began to wind down just as Louise noticed Edie gearing up for one of her ranting discourses. Louise quickly but firmly changed the subject. Maggie was feeling bad enough without them harping on Jon Hunter's death or the incidence of crime in the suburbs. After all, they had no information, except the fact that a man was dead. So, as they put the last pin into the quilt sandwich and pulled up chairs to begin the quilting, Louise asked Maggie about Hal's family vacation.

"Have you heard from him since they left?"

"Oh, yes." Maggie brightened as she told of the phone conversation she'd had with her grandsons over the weekend. "They had so much fun at Disneyland they could hardly talk fast enough. They're leaving for San Diego tomorrow, to see the zoo and Sea World."

Anna began to reminisce about a trip to Disneyland she'd taken with her grandkids, which led to other such memories. Within a short time, however, inevitably, the conversation returned to Jonathan Hunter.

"Imagine knowing a Broadway star." Clare sighed.

"Imagine knowing a person who's been murdered."

Maggie thought Edie said this with more relish than dread. And she noticed that Anna couldn't suppress the small shudder that shook her shoulders.

"I read a book once where the understudy killed the star so he could take over the lead," Clare commented. Her eyes sparkled. Most of the others also enjoyed reading mysteries and understood her interest.

"He wasn't a Broadway star, Clare," Maggie reminded her. "He had the lead in the Los Angeles production of *Phantom of the Opera* and was starring in the tour. I don't see how it would be worth murdering someone to star in the touring production."

Maggie, feeling more like herself now that the initial shock was past, couldn't help noticing the spark of excitement in Clare. She thought it ironic that she was now so enthusiastic about getting involved in solving this crime. Less than an hour before she had been willing to give up her daily walks on the off chance that she might discover a body lying in the street. Maggie felt a smile tugging at the corners of her mouth. Clare liked to imagine herself as another Jessica Fletcher, but Maggie knew she would cringe at even one dead body in her path. Clare wanted her murders done tidily offstage as they were in the "cozy" mysteries she preferred.

Clare's mind was still on her beloved books and their plots. "Wouldn't it be exciting if we could solve it ourselves—the way the woman in the book did? In fact"—Clare stopped stitching to turn toward Maggie and Victoria—"the woman in the book was a volunteer with the theater group. She knew everyone in the theater and the production and she figured out who the murderer was before the police did."

Everyone looked at Maggie and Victoria. Stitching virtually stopped. Touring Broadway shows played in the valley at the Gammage Auditorium on the campus of Arizona State University in Tempe. Like many large theaters, the Gammage relied on volunteers to serve as ushers during their shows and other events. And Maggie and Victoria were two of their volunteers.

"You two could find out all about it and tell us all the details. You always tell us about the shows you see there anyway." Clare's eyes sparkled with the possibilities. "Oh, I wish I was a volunteer there myself. Maybe I'll sign up."

"You probably wouldn't be able to start right away," Victoria warned her. "There are a lot of volunteers, and waiting lists for more. I'm sure the police will have solved this long before you work your first show."

Clare looked disappointed but refused to give up on her hope of solving a real crime. "But do you and Victoria get to meet the actors and get to know them?"

"No."

Clare looked so disappointed at Maggie's short reply that Victoria sought to soften her disappointment. "The paid workers at the Gammage often hear things about the shows and actors and they pass the information along." She explained to the others that in addition to the volunteers, there were a number of paid floor managers who were students at Arizona State. "We volunteers just work out in the lobby and auditorium, but the floor managers work at the stage door, so they get to meet the actors there. Especially with a show with a long run like *Phantom of the Opera,* they're sure to have something to say. It's only been playing for a week, though, and we only worked the one night. But we didn't hear anything negative. In fact, everyone said how really nice the actors are."

"Who's the understudy?" Clare wanted to know.

"According to an article I read in the paper," Victoria told them, "Jonathan Hunter played André before taking on the lead. And he understudied the Phantom role. I'll bring my playbill from the show tomorrow if you'd like to see it. It lists the understudies."

Clare thanked her and turned her attention back to her stitching. They sat around the frame in the small, brightly lit room, the feather pattern in the quilt border magically appearing beneath their skilled fingers. Maggie noted the glow of interest that the unsolved mystery put in the eyes of her friends. She had to admit it preoccupied her as well. Could they actually solve a mystery themselves, just by discussing it over the quilt frame? Maggie considered this as her needle worked its way in and out of the quilt. Well, why not? They were intelligent women with a variety of experiences behind them. Every morning, over the quilt frame, they discussed a diverse range of topics. Current events were always popular, especially local issues and events. They spoke of taxes and finances, of trusts and estate planning. And, perhaps most important of all in this instance, they passed around murder mysteries, then dissected the plots. The more Maggie thought it over, the more the idea appealed to her. And wouldn't her son Michael be surprised if they could come up with a suspect?

That afternoon, Maggie stepped out of her condo, deep in thought. She was dressed in her comfortable old jeans and a worn cotton work shirt that had been her husband's, the sleeves rolled up to her elbows. Scuffed boots were on her feet and a straw hat in her hands. Her mind was so far away that she almost bumped into Victoria before her brain registered the presence of the other woman.

"Victoria! What are you doing here?" Maggie was so surprised to see her friend on her doorstep she didn't even consider how abrupt her words sounded.

But Victoria, used to her friend's forthright way, wasn't offended. "I just thought you might like some company. And I wanted a little walk."

Maggie smiled, giving Victoria an impulsive hug. They'd met a few years ago at a get-together in their condominium's community room. An instant friendship formed when they discovered a common interest in quilting, and Maggie soon had Victoria, a Lutheran, attending the St. Rose Quilting Bee.

"Thank you. But I'm just leaving for the ranch. Hal has old Jimmy out there to feed the animals and all, but I like to go over and make sure everything is all right. And to water Sara's houseplants."

Victoria smiled. "And while you're there you'll have a nice ride on Chestnut."

Maggie had to laugh. "Can't fool you for a minute." She waved her hat as she talked. "Why else would I offer to look after things while they're gone? I'm still attached to that old horse. I admit it." Her eyes clouded over for a moment. "I'm especially looking forward to my ride today. It helps clear my mind. Lets me think."

"You can use that today," Victoria agreed. "It's a perfect day for riding." As she waved her friend off she couldn't help adding, "Take care now."

Chapter Two

The hot sun poured down on Maggie's back. She always enjoyed a long ride on Chestnut. The original HB Ranch had shrunk when Maggie and Harry sold part of their property to help finance the boys' educations. But the rest of the Browne property had been kept intact all these years, boasting many acres and accessing the mountain preserve area to the north.

But now Hal wanted to sell off more of the old ranch, retaining mainly the house and enough land to enable him to keep a few horses. Hal, a contract lawyer, no longer raised the horses his father had so loved, but he did keep a stable of horses for the family to ride—something he wanted to continue to do. The place just wouldn't be the same without the horses.

When Maggie and Harry were raising their family, the area had been county land. Now it was part of the booming northern Scottsdale market. At current prices the land would bring in a great deal of money, which Hal planned to share with the entire Browne family. The money was especially needed by Hal's younger brother, Bobby, whose wife was pregnant with their first child. Bobby and his wife were both teachers; the money could make a real difference for them. Hal was pretending to be overwhelmed by the work involved in the upkeep of the large property; he didn't want his brother to feel like a charity case, or to leave him plagued with guilt over the loss of the family land.

Maggie was very proud of her son, yet it saddened her to think that this land would soon be gone. There were memories here, links to the self she'd been as a bride, young wife, and new mother. She could feel Harry's presence here, could almost hear the voices of her young sons. And it still brought her peace to ride out into the undisturbed desert.

A ground squirrel scampered across the hard-packed soil of the trail before her, making Maggie smile. Maggie loved her comfortable condo and enjoyed its proximity to the city, but she did miss the wildlife. Although they were all shy of humans, out here she would often glimpse the little ground squirrels, as well as coyotes, rabbits, roadrunners, hawks, and numerous other birds. Lizards were a common sight; javelinas and snakes, thank goodness, were more rare.

She was coming to the end of the Browne property, but decided to continue on through some open desert into the mountains. There were some old trails there still used by the horse owners who lived in the area. As the small ranches were sold and became upscale subdivisions, there were less and less horse properties around. Just enough new developments retained the horse ownership rights to keep the flavor of the area. Maggie found herself drawn to the past here. Although progress was inevitable, she regretted the way it changed the old comfortable and familiar areas of her youth.

A twitch of Chestnut's head and a dog's bark brought Maggie out of her reverie and back to the present. A hundred or so feet away, she spotted a tall man, his shoulders stooped, his clothes rumpled and none too clean-looking. He had a dog with him, a large animal with hunting blood in him, probably several different types. At the moment, he remained quiet at his owner's side, but he kept vigilant eyes on Maggie and her mount.

Maggie halted Chestnut, keeping alert so that she could leave at once if the stranger proved dangerous. She'd brought a cell phone with her, but it was in her saddlebag along with a snack, and not readily accessible. Something to remember in the future, she decided, patting Chestnut's neck to calm them both. Concentrating on holding a relaxed stance, she looked over at the man.

Who could be wandering way out here, wearing clothes like those and with a scruffy dog? Was it a homeless man? She hadn't heard of any transients camping in the area, though it was certainly a possibility. Many of the homeless owned dogs. But it was cold at night in the desert at this time of year, and the area was dotted with expensive homes equipped with the latest in security systems. It seemed unlikely someone would choose to camp out here or that he'd remain long once seen and reported. She hadn't seen any type of structure where he could get in out of the cold or escape the hot sun. Not even a sleeping roll tucked under a sheltering shrub.

"Well, if it ain't Maggie Browne."

The gravelly voice stirred a memory that had Maggie squinting at the sun-browned face now turned toward her. The man wore an old hat that may have once been an expensive Stetson; it shaded his face and covered most of his hair. She could see that the latter was graying and long, and that there was some gray in the stubble of his beard.

"Harley?" She finally identified the unique voice as that of a neighbor. "Harley Stoner?"

"Yep." He walked closer. "Well, haven't seen you for a coon's age, Maggie Browne. Looking out for your son's place, I expect."

"Yes." Maggie had to concentrate to prevent answering "yep" to match his manner of speech. "I take it you know they're out of town. Jimmy looks after the animals, but I like to come over and visit Chestnut."

Her former neighbor nodded, looking over the horse with a critical eye. "She looks good. Must be getting old, though. Like the rest of us."

"She's a good horse," Maggie said, patting her mount on the neck. "How have you been, Harley?"

As the words left her mouth, Maggie frowned, wishing she could call them back. Harley, she suddenly remembered, was one of those people you should never question, even casually, about health. He generally took such questions seriously and went into detailed descriptions of his most recent ailments. Rheumatism had bothered him for years and he was also beset with intestinal problems that were better left out of social conversations. Braced for a long session of listening, Maggie was surprised when his only reply to her inquiry was a shrug and an offhand remark.

"Been better. Rheumatism, you know."

Chestnut stood quietly during the moment of silence that followed. Maggie almost wished for a less docile animal—a high-spirited horse who danced about impatiently would have required her attention and given her an excuse to move on. But Chestnut waited patiently for her rider's next command, quietly nibbling at some scrubby growth at the side of the trail.

"Heard about that Hunter boy?"

Maggie could have fallen from the saddle, she was so surprised. Harley had always been one to keep to himself. She was amazed that he remembered Jon at all, much less knew about his murder.

"Yes. It's such a shame. I remember him as a sweet little boy." Maggie sighed. "I saw him perform last week and he was very good. Such a beautiful voice." A wistful note sounded in her voice, regret at such talent cut short in so tragic a manner.

"Hmph. Durn fool actor."

Maggie was ready to ride away in disgust when his next remark brought her up short.

"Killed right over the hill there, you know." He nodded ahead of them, toward the mountain, where the softly rolling terrain grew steeper. The ground was hard and rocky, though rain earlier in the season provided a scattering of yellow and orange wildflowers. Blooming brittlebrush, bright yellow in the afternoon sun, a few deceptively fluffy-looking chollas, and one diseased saguaro led to the knoll Harley indicated.

The sun continued to shine warmly on her back, but Maggie's body turned chilly. She felt ill, looking toward the spot, knowing how close it was to Hal's. Another hundred feet and it would have been on his property. What had led the murderer here to this spot? And was there any chance of his returning, making his way to the nearby ranch house where Hal, Sara, and their young sons would soon be back in residence?

Maggie pulled herself together. She shouldn't be thinking this way; it would make her crazy.

But what was it Harley had said? Could he know something no one else knew? "How do you know he was killed there?"

Harley shrugged. "Stands to reason. Found the body there, didn't they?"

So he didn't know anything after all, he was making assumptions.

Harley looked after his dog, who had decided Chestnut was not a danger and moved off to sniff under some greasewood, busily tracking a rabbit or a lizard. Still turned away from Maggie, so that she had to strain to hear him, he made his next remark. "That Hunter was a real good-for-nothing."

Maggie considered just riding away. "What do you mean? Jon was only a boy when they left here." Her voice reflected her indignation. "And he was one of the sweetest children I'd ever met. He was always over at our place, you know, playing with my boys."

"Don't mean him. Talking about Ed Hunter. Never knew the boy much."

Maggie frowned. So he was referring to Jon's father. "I didn't have much contact with Ed. But Carmen was a lovely woman and a devoted mother. Jon always came to our place to play because she worked part-time over at the school."

Harley nodded his agreement, an almost pleasant look on his face. Then he seemed to recollect himself and pasted his habitual scowl back in place.

Maggie barely noticed Harley's reaction to her words as she settled her hands on the saddle horn. Her lips pulled together into a thin line as she tried to remember more about the family. There had been rumors about Ed and his treatment of his family. She decided to be noncommittal. "I met Ed, of course, when we had neighborhood get-togethers. Did you know him well, then?"

"Knew him some. Ornery guy."

Harley suddenly seemed anxious to retrieve his dog, who had stopped sniffing at the bush and had started digging. He moved away from Maggie and Chestnut, calling in his gruff voice, "Come on, boy. Git on out of there and let's git on home."

Without even a wave he started off at a brisk trot. Maggie stared after him and "Boy" for a minute before she continued her ride. Harley was a character. For as long as she'd known him, he'd always had a dog of some kind, and all he ever called it was "Boy." She wondered if they were registered under that name at Animal Control.

But then, what was she thinking? Harley probably never bought a license for a dog in his entire life!

The humor left her face and her lips set in a grim line as she topped the low hill Harley had pointed out to her. She brought Chestnut to a halt and stared ahead.

The crime scene.

Maggie didn't know what she'd expected, but this small swatch of desert wasn't it. Yellow plastic tape fluttered in a warm breeze, roping off a roughly square area as it stretched from shrub to tree to saguaro. One lone police car was parked at the side of the access road, a bored-looking officer sitting behind the wheel and reading some papers. Probably stationed there to keep away the curious, like herself.

Except for the crime scene tape and the police car, it all looked so ordinary. The wildflowers bloomed, their orange and yellow faces turned up to the sun in silent worship. A ground squirrel sat up, his eyes searching the area before he scampered across the dusty soil, his tail an exclamation point that finally disappeared into the earth. A hawk soared overhead, riding the air currents, its large body moving in a graceful swirl.

Or was it a vulture?

Maggie stared at the dark shape for a moment before deciding that she really couldn't tell. Blinking against the brightness of the sun, she moved her gaze to a huge, strangely shaped saguaro. With its four large arms, it must have stood in this spot for over two hundred years. If only it could talk, what a history it could tell! Of Native Americans and prospectors, of hunters and the hunted. And, perhaps, of murder—of its victim and its perpetrator.

Chapter Three

Maggie watched the news that evening with an intentness she usually reserved for designing a new quilt top or solving one of her mystery novels. As she prepared dinner for her son Michael, Maggie watched the frenzy of competition that the murder of Jonathan Hunter was creating among local reporters. There were interviews with other members of the company, with the stage crew, with musicians from the orchestra. Station helicopters flew over the mountains to show the area where the body was found. Maggie stared at the familiar contours of the desert, marred only by police vehicles and bright yellow tape. She wondered how the neighbors in that exclusive area felt about the media invasion. Hal's area. What a relief he was away.

To Maggie's surprise, the interviews on one station included a talk with Michael's former third grade teacher. He and Jon had been in the same class that year. How had the reporter ever discovered this small elderly woman who had taught third grade for most of her life? Maggie knew she'd been retired for many years; she remembered attending her retirement party with Michael when he was in the sixth grade. And Michael was a man now.

"He was such a sweet little boy," Mrs. Fitzgerald was saying. "I went to see him right away when I heard he was playing the Phantom. I waited outside afterward and he was so nice to me. He always was a nice, polite little boy."

In response to a question from the reporter, she elaborated on his days in the classroom. "It didn't surprise me at all that he was the lead in this play. Even as a boy he had a nice voice. And he liked to sing. That's the important thing. A lot of little boys are too shy or embarrassed to sing at that age. But little Jon was always ready for a solo. Even in third grade, he had a nice stage presence."

Maggie turned off the set when the doorbell rang. The station was cutting to a commercial anyway.

As she walked to the door to let Michael in, she could see little Jon sitting in her kitchen with her sons, leading them in a song. He'd been a small child physically, with a slight build. But he did love to sing—more than anything. The memories of him came so easily. How could he be grown, singing in a Broadway show? And now dead. Murdered. It was more than a body could cope with.

And how was Michael taking the death of his old friend? As a police officer, Michael was used to facing death. But this was a special circumstance, and Maggie worried about him. He might be thirty-one-years-old now, but he was still her baby.

In this strange mood of equal parts nostalgia, grief, and motherly love, Maggie opened the door. She was immediately engulfed in the gruffly loving hug of her youngest son. Tall, robust, and muscular, he held Maggie in a silent greeting that spoke volumes. Michael, her only son still a bachelor, came to dinner every Monday evening, and Maggie was delighted that he hadn't called to cancel. Even with silence, they could connect tonight. Maggie knew Michael was recalling the same little boy she'd been remembering all day.

She held on to him, both taking and giving comfort. When they finally parted, Maggie led the way into her kitchen where dinner was already on the table. She'd made all of Michael's favorite dishes. She supposed she was being the stereotypical mother and offering him comfort through food. Not that food could make up for the loss of a friend. She'd even thought of using the small dining room, but felt it would be too formal for their weekly meal.

Tonight, comfort mattered above all. And if Michael wanted to talk about Jon, well . . . Maggie was more than willing to listen.

"Go on, sit down," Maggie urged.

But Michael stood beside the heavily laden table, staring at all his favorite foods. "You made all this special, didn't you? To make me feel better." He leaned over and placed a kiss on his mother's cheek.

Maggie blushed. She had meant to make him feel better if he was upset about his old friend. But she'd also hoped to ease some information from him. Although the body had been found far from Michael's patrol area, he was still a police officer in Scottsdale. An old friend of his had been killed. He must have heard *something* that hadn't been on television.

Trying not to look guilty, she cut a wedge of lasagna and put it on his plate. "Here you go. You must be hungry." She sat down before adding a smaller serving to her own plate.

"Actually, I wasn't. Until now. This looks great, Ma."

Silence reigned for a moment as they filled their plates and sampled the food. Finally, Maggie broached the subject that hovered at the forefront of both their minds.

"You know, Victoria and I saw Jonathan perform last week. Two of our friends had to cancel and asked us to usher in their place."

"We didn't keep up a lot these last couple of years, but I'm going to miss him." Michael shook his head regretfully as he filled his fork with lasagna. "I wish we'd been able to get together before this happened. We were supposed to, you know, but I had to work late that day. A big accident just as the shift was changing. Jon was over at my place—that's when he left the tickets for us. But he couldn't stay until I got back."

Maggie looked at her youngest son. "You two were very close once, even if it was a long time ago."

Michael nodded, but Maggie was glad to see him resume his eating. It took a lot to kill a young man's appetite. She'd counted on that fact and the power of his favorite dishes to lull him into a comfortable, slightly distracted state.

"The thing that hurt me most was hearing from Hal."

Maggie gave him a quizzical look.

"So he didn't call you." Michael put his fork down and shook his head. "If you've been puzzling over this, wait until you hear this. Jon went over to Hal's that week before the show opened. To look at the land he has up for sale."

Maggie couldn't suppress a comment. "He did?"

"Hal didn't recognize him and Jon must have gotten a kick out of playing a part and stringing him along. Told him he'd lived in the area as a child, that he had a pretty good job now and he was interested in buying some land. Maybe building a house. He asked about having horses on the property. He managed to go on for a long time without giving his full name. Hal had no idea it was Jon. Then when he finally had to give his full name he asked Hal to keep it to himself. Wanted to surprise me with the news or something." Michael shook his head. "I don't know when he planned to tell me, because he never said a word when we talked last week."

Maggie also thought this was odd behavior for the boy she remembered. "I'm sure he would have told you when we all saw the show this Friday. The show has five more weeks to run, so there would have been a lot of time available for you two to get together."

Michael shrugged. "We'll never know."

He finished his lasagna, helping himself to more from the casserole dish on the table. "So . . . is all of this meant as comfort food or were you hoping to pump something out of me with this feast?" His voice was scolding, but his eyes were loving. He was joking with her. And he was definitely enjoying the food.

"Honestly, you're so suspicious. It must come from being a cop." But she was smiling.

Michael just raised one eyebrow as he brought his fork to his mouth. "It also comes from knowing you."

It was Maggie's turn to shrug. "Well, the news anchors don't seem to have any information, and I thought you might know something. . . ."

"Ma. You know I can't talk about ongoing cases."

Maggie was quick to placate him. "I know that, dear. I just thought—him being your old friend and all—that you might have some news you could share with the family."

Michael had to smile at his mother. She was really something. "Like what?"

"What was he doing out there at that hour of the night?"

Michael finished up the food on his plate, pushing it away with a satisfied grin on his face. "Honestly, Ma, no one can make lasagna like you."

Maggie smiled her thanks, wondering if she should push him to answer her question. He was probably just teasing her, making her work hard to find out what little bits of information he could tell her.

"Did you make dessert?"

Maggie laughed, rising from her chair to take a cake keeper from the counter. "Would I make your favorite dinner and forget the devil's-food cake?"

Michael's grin lit up his face and Maggie wondered again how he'd managed to stay single for so long. So good-looking and with a pleasant personality.

But the imp kept her wondering about the answer to her question about Jon until he'd finished two slices of cake.

"Actually, this case is out of my area, but I did try to find out what actually happened out there as soon as I heard about it. Not only because it was Jon, but because it's so close to Hal's."

"I know." Her brows drew together with worry even as she felt better about her concern. Here she'd been scolding herself for the gnawing anxiety she felt about her oldest son and his family, and it turned out her practical youngest son, the cop, was also worried. Hal and his family were returning soon and she hoped they would feel safe in their home.

"The thing about that area is, it's popular with the kids for weekend parties. You know that. So there are all kinds of tire tracks and footprints. No one knows why Jon was out there. Or, if they do, they're not talking."

Michael sipped from his mug of coffee. "Since I heard from Hal, I've been wondering if Jon had an urge to look at the property after the show, drove out there, and someone followed him out and stole the car. It's an unusual area for a carjacking, but these things do happen. Especially so late at night, when there's so little traffic."

Maggie frowned at the thought of criminals so close to Hal's. But Michael was still talking.

"Some gang members could have spotted him driving up Mill Avenue, decided they liked the car, and followed him out to northeast Scottsdale. I referred Hal to the detective in charge of the case, but he'll have to stop in and talk to him again as soon as he gets back."

Maggie nodded as she listened. "That makes a lot of sense." It also made her feel better about the danger, or lack thereof, around Hal's house.

Michael was still talking, thinking out loud. "It would have been pretty late when Jon got out there, too, meaning there wouldn't have been many cars on the road. A large group of actors stopped at Mi Casa restaurant for a late dinner after the show."

Maggie grabbed at this crumb of information—not mentioning it in case it was a slip on his part. His theory satisfied Maggie's curiosity somewhat, even supported her own, but it didn't relieve her anxiety about Hal's family and their safety.

"So you don't think Hal and his family are in any danger? If it was a carjacker?"

Michael shook his head. "Right now it looks like a crime of opportunity. Some kids probably saw the car on the main road, followed him out there, and couldn't believe their luck when he stopped the car. To look around or whatever. The thing is, if some kids stole it, it could be in another state or down in Mexico by now, or broken up into a million parts. They would have wanted to get some quick money out of it."

"So this wasn't just a case of joyriding."

Michael shook his head. Sitting back comfortably in his chair, he leaned back until only the rear legs touched the floor. "If it was, we'll find the car soon. In Tempe or Chandler, maybe, or on the Indian reservation. In a canal. They usually turn up within a few days."

He accepted the cup of coffee she handed him with a grateful nod. "We may never know what really happened to Jon, Ma."

But Maggie's mind was still busy turning over possibilities. "Maybe he was taking someone out to see the property," Maggie suggested.

"If he did, it seems likely it was someone from the cast, and in that case, no one's admitting it."

"Do you know where Jon was staying in the valley? You talked to him after he arrived."

"Leave it alone, Ma. The detective in charge of the case is an excellent man and if there's a solution he'll find it."

Maggie wanted to ask more. But she recognized that look on Michael's face. He was done with this topic and she knew she'd never get him back to it. With a pleasant smile for her son, but an interior sigh of frustration, Maggie rose and began to clear the table.

Chapter Four

After Michael left, Maggie busied herself with cleaning up. Sweet son that he was, he'd offered to help. But she knew he'd put in a long day patrolling the streets of Scottsdale. She could see his eyelids beginning to droop even as he finished a second cup of coffee. She wanted to put him in the spare room, but instead sent him home with orders to play the radio *loudly* in the car. Besides, she hoped the work involved in cleaning up the messy pots and pans would keep her mind off subjects better set aside.

But of course, that hope was futile. As she rinsed out the lasagna pan, she thought of her four sons. They were all good boys, men now, of course, but still boys to her mind. Hal was a busy contract lawyer, yet he spent all his off hours keeping up the old ranch. His boys helped, of course, but they were young and busy with their friends, school activities, and sports. And he had old Jimmy who'd been there since Harry and Maggie's day.

Frank was a local vet. He helped Hal with the family horses, even though he specialized in small animals. Frank and his wife April were the parents of the only girl in the Browne family in three generations, Maggie's dear granddaughter Megan.

And Bobby. He taught fifth grade. Just last year he'd married another teacher at the same school. Merrie taught second grade. They were looking forward to the birth of their baby. Maggie knew they would be wonderful parents.

And of course there was Michael. Maggie had always tried not to play favorites, but there was something special about a woman's youngest child. And Michael had always been such a sweet and charming child. Much like Jon.

Jon. He had been Carmen's *only* child. Her baby. Maggie wondered how she was managing. Carmen had been a pretty young woman, always eager to help out with school or church activities. But she was quiet and shy, difficult to know. She was a hard worker, taking a job in the school cafeteria in order to pay for music lessons for her son. They'd been friends all those years ago, though not close ones. They'd exchanged letters for a while and then Christmas cards for a little longer. But then, as often happened, Maggie lost touch with her. Her heart bled for Carmen now. Losing a child had to be the most difficult thing in the world.

Maggie had just finished drying her hands when the sharp jangle of the phone startled her.

"Maggie Browne?" The voice at the other end of the telephone was female, soft-pitched and tentative.

"Yes." Maggie's voice, too, was uncertain. She didn't recognize the voice, yet telephone solicitors wouldn't ask for "Maggie." And there was something vaguely familiar about the soft-edged voice.

"This is Carmen Hunter. I don't know if you remember me."

"Carmen Hunter!" Maggie's voice raised in pleasure and surprise. First Harley, and now Carmen. She would never pull herself out of the nostalgic mood that was gripping her with these old acquaintances coming forward again after so many years. And to think she'd just been reminiscing about Carmen!

"Of course I remember you. I've been thinking about you. I am *so* sorry about Jon."

"Thank you." Carmen's voice became even quieter, making Maggie struggle to hear her. "He was such a good son."

"He was always a sweet boy." Maggie sighed. There was so little you could say to a mother who had just lost her son. "I've gotten nostalgic these past weeks, thinking a lot about the times when my boys were young. I don't know what started it . . . getting old I guess. But Jon was such an intrinsic part of that time, I can't help thinking about him, too. I was so happy to hear he was coming to the valley. I was going to have him out for a home-cooked meal. . . ."

Her voice trailed off and she waited for Carmen to make a response. After some thirty seconds of silence she began to feel uncomfortable, clearing her throat to create some noise. But still Carmen remained silent. Finally, she felt a need to speak.

"Uh . . . he gave Michael some tickets, you know. So that all of us could go to see him perform. They're for this coming Friday."

Still Carmen was silent, and Maggie wondered if she was trying to bring herself under control. Yet she didn't hear any sobbing from the other end. Although she had an appearance of fragility, Maggie had always felt Carmen was a strong woman. Perhaps she had been wrong.

Maggie was searching her mind for something more to say when Carmen finally broke the silence.

"Maggie . . . I know it's been along time. But I remember how together you always were, even with all those little boys. Sometimes I had trouble coping with just the one and there you were with your four. And mine making five half the time. You were always so organized and so competent about everything."

She stopped for a moment and Maggie wondered what on earth she was leading up to.

"I remember that time when Jon was in third grade, when someone was stealing the kids' lunch money. You just got right in there and discovered what was going on. Got that little guy signed up for the free lunch program, so he didn't have to steal to eat."

Maggie had forgotten all about the incident Carmen mentioned. Apparently it made a much greater impression on Carmen than it did on her.

Carmen's voice broke. "Maggie, I know we haven't really kept in touch . . . and it's been a long time. But I always thought of you as someone who could do anything, face anything. And I wondered if I could borrow some of your strength."

Maggie could hear the other woman suck in a shaky breath. There were long pauses between her sentences and Maggie wondered if she was wiping her eyes. "Oh, Carmen, of course I'll help. What is it?"

"I'm in Phoenix. I've been here for over a week."

"You're here?" Maggie was so surprised her voice rose.

Something that could have been either a sigh or a sniffle came over the line. "I came to be near Jon. I don't get to see him much since he started touring."

Maggie waited. She had the impression Carmen meant to say more, but she must have changed her mind. Either that or Maggie was imagining things.

Maggie heard some noises that she thought indicated Carmen was sipping a drink, then her voice came back on, sounding stronger.

"The reason I called . . . I've talked to the police. They were very nice and came here to tell me—" Her voice broke.

Maggie knew they must have come in person to tell her about Jon. She wondered how they'd known where to find her, but it didn't seem appropriate to ask.

"But they want to talk to me again. About Jon's life, they said. His friends, his enemies."

"Well, that makes a lot of sense," Maggie said. "They'll be looking for people who might have a motive for killing him."

Carmen's voice rose to a near-hysterical pitch. "But he was such a good boy. Who could possibly want to kill him?"

"Carmen, you have to pull yourself together." Maggie didn't want to sound harsh, but Carmen was sounding too near hysteria for her own good.

As for her refusal to believe Jon had any enemies—Maggie knew she would feel exactly the same about any of her own sons. But in this case she was more objective. Jon probably wasn't as "good" as his mother wanted to believe. He was dead and someone had killed him. Deliberately. It had been many years since he was the sweet little boy she remembered. In that time it was very possible he'd met at least one person who disliked him.

Maggie's words seemed to help. Carmen's voice was more even when she spoke again.

"I just wondered . . . I have to go in and talk to them. And I also have to find out about claiming the body."

Her voice broke again and Maggie's heart went out to her. But she was still very surprised at Carmen's request when it came.

"Maggie, would you go with me?"

"To the police station?"

"Yes. In Scottsdale. To find out about how to make the arrangements. I don't have any family here and I just don't know if I can handle it on my own."

Maggie didn't know what else to say. "Why, of course I will."

"I thought of asking Michael. I know he's a policeman. But I haven't seen him since he was a little boy and I didn't think I could ask him." Her voice grew softer. "And I thought another woman would understand."

After further assurances that Carmen was not imposing and that she would be glad to help, Maggie hung up the phone. For a moment she remained seated at the kitchen table, staring ahead at nothing. Then she pulled herself together and pushed out of the straight wooden chair. She rarely felt old, but tonight she did. Perhaps a soak in a hot tub would not be amiss.

She walked slowly to the refrigerator to fill a mug with milk. She'd heat it in the microwave and hope the natural properties of the warm milk would help her sleep. It was past her bedtime, yet her mind was churning like an excited four-year-old's on Christmas Eve.

The milk didn't help. An hour later, Maggie's thoughts still swept around and around. Though she tried to empty her mind and sleep, she continued to hear snatches of song in Jon's beautiful voice—songs from *Phantom of the Opera.* Even before his death, ever since she'd seen him perform, the music had followed her through the day—songs of dreams and love, of music and freedom. But now it twisted her heart to realize that the sweet boy she'd known would no longer be able to dream or sing.

Maggie turned over, raising her head high enough to turn and fluff her pillow. What had gotten into her lately? It wasn't just the terrible death of a young man she'd known years before. Recently, she'd been plagued by thoughts of her earlier life. The good times with Harry, the years when the children were young. Having her granddaughter Megan over for the weekend had brought recurring thoughts of her boys when they were the same age. So long ago. And now Jon's death brought more scenes to dance around in her mind. He'd been such an integral part of their lives in those early years.

And tonight, Carmen. Speaking with her this evening reawakened memories of the small, quiet woman. And raised questions. What was she doing in Phoenix? She'd apparently been with Jon the whole time. Was their relationship as wonderful as she indicated?

Maggie turned again. How could she let herself question a mother's love for her son? Everything was just getting to be too much; her poor brain couldn't cope.

She flipped over onto her back, thinking with a sigh that Harry would have been very upset with her for all the tossing and turning. It had always taken her longer to fall asleep and he often complained that she couldn't keep still. If only he were here now, to hold her still and share his warmth and comfort.

Maggie knew what the problem was; she just didn't want to admit it. She was getting old. Harry was gone. The boys had lives of their own, children of their own. She was feeling unnecessary. Unneeded.

It was the breaking of the old ranch property that triggered all these old memories. Oh, she understood why Hal was doing it. Bobby and Merrie would need every penny they could get from their share of the ranch sale money. And Maggie didn't begrudge them the right to help their child. But it was still difficult. It brought back all these memories of earlier times. Of the kids. Of she and Harry as newlyweds. Riding together. The hard work. The difficult times. The enjoyable times. The excitement of that first pregnancy. Bringing home the boys. Teaching them to ride. Yes, they'd had a lot of fun in their lives.

Jonathan Hunter was a part of that time. Her boys had loved to have friends over. The house and yard were always full of their friends. Who wouldn't like to come over and ride their horses? And play with the dogs and cats they'd always had? Jonathan had been Michael's best friend for many years.

Maggie rolled over again, trying to find a comfortable spot in the rumpled bed. Those days were over, and would never be again. Times had changed. Scottsdale had changed. Hal would make an enormous amount of money for the family on this deal, and Bobby and his unborn child would benefit. But the family home—the one that filled her memories and often her dreams—would never be the same. The house would still be there, but most of the rest of it would be gone. The fields where they'd ridden and played cowboy. Where the boys had raised their own steers and tried their hand at growing vegetables. Where they'd built shelters of palm fronds and ocotillo stems and camped out overnight. The little creek that ran through the pasture when it rained, where they'd had many a picnic over the years.

Maggie changed position once again, pulling the sheet firmly over her. With her right hand, she reached into the drawer of her nightstand. Within moments, her head rested easier on the pillow, her hand tucked in beside her, fingering the familiar beads of her turquoise rosary. A wedding gift from Harry, the rosary was one of her most treasured possessions. Reciting the age-old prayers with this rosary was a guaranteed way to bring her comfort.

As her fingers slipped over the cool beads, a feeling of peace washed over her, and she finally fell into a dreamless sleep.

Chapter Five

At the Quilting Bee the next morning, talk once again centered around Jonathan Hunter. According to the local media, the police had no leads. Reporters tried to speculate but couldn't even come up with a reasonable explanation for why he was found in that particular area. It was not far enough out in the desert for it to be a place to dump a body, but in an upscale neighborhood filled with homes equipped with security systems. And the old stand-by that a transient or gang had done it didn't work either, as that area was not frequented by them. Why would a homeless person be so far outside the city where the services he needed were available? And the upscale neighborhood was notably lacking in gang activity.

To make up for the lack of solid information, the television stations played up the local connection and searched for former friends and associates of Jonathan to interview. All of these sounded remarkably similar. Everyone said he was a wonderful person. He was nice to the other actors. He was always willing to participate in charity events. No one could think of any reason why someone would want to kill him.

"Why would he have been out there so late?" Edie wanted to know. "Asking for trouble, if you ask me."

"What time does the show end?" Clare asked.

"Could he have been staying with someone who lived out there?" Anna's question was tentative.

Victoria and Maggie could answer some of the questions. They had worked the show and knew that it usually ended at 10:30. On Sundays it ended at 10:00 because it started at 7:30 instead of 8:00. And Victoria remembered hearing that companies coming for long runs, like *Phantom of the Opera,* were housed in apartments in the area. But she didn't know where those might be. All the apartments around the university itself would certainly be filled during the school year and there were no apartments in the vicinity of the mountain where he was found. Besides, the mountains of northern Scottsdale were a long way from the theater in Tempe, a fact which Maggie pointed out.

"But since he lived here years ago, he might have had friends who invited him to stay," Anna insisted.

Maggie had to agree that Anna's theory had merit. "Still, Michael kept in touch with him for years and I never heard that anyone else did. And he didn't have many friends as a child. I never knew why, but Michael seemed to be his only close friend. He was one of those children who seemed to get along better with adults than with other children." Maggie tucked her thread within the quilt layers and clipped it, hiding the ends inside the batting. She reached for the spool of thread.

"But with him being a leading actor now, you never know," Clare stated. "People like to associate with someone like that. And a lot of those houses on the mountain have separate guest houses, which would be just the thing for a guest who had to work late every night."

"Those large, expensive homes with the guest houses are new," Maggie pointed out. "When he lived here, all that land was either desert, or small ranches like ours. Or smaller, inexpensive homes for the ranch hands like the one the Hunters lived in."

They worked in silence for a while, thinking their separate thoughts while the needles plunged in and out of the cotton fabric. Work on the Grandmother's Fan quilt was proceeding well and they were almost ready to readjust the frames, rolling the already-worked borders so that they could get at the unstitched area further in.

"I wonder if Michael knows where he was staying." Maggie's voice was speculative.

"That's right," Louise said. "Monday is your regular night to make dinner for him, isn't it? Then he did come last night?"

"Yes, he did. And he seems to be taking it well." Maggie continued to set her small, even stitches into the quilt.

"Did you find out anything about the case that wasn't in the paper?" Clare wanted to know.

"There wasn't *anything* in the paper," Edie grumbled.

"Well, he did mention that the actors all went to dinner after the show. At Mi Casa. It must have been late by the time they finished and left."

Maggie smoothed her fingers over the stitches she'd just set, checking that the tension was right. As she readjusted her glasses and returned to her stitching, she made a mild comment that hit the group like a splash of cold water on a chilly winter day. "Darn, I wish I'd thought to ask Carmen where he was staying when she called last night. And I didn't think to get her number."

As she paused, tugging at her thread to release a snarl, Maggie realized the others were staring at her. Clare's mouth was actually hanging open.

Maggie hadn't even mentioned to Victoria on the drive in that morning that Carmen had called. She didn't know why. After the stunned silence that followed her pronouncement, she wondered if she should have mentioned it now. Then everyone began talking at once. It took a moment for them to settle back down.

"You talked to Carmen Hunter last night?" Victoria finally asked.

Maggie felt bad. Victoria sounded hurt. She really should have told her about the call in the car this morning.

"I should have told you earlier, but I've had so much on my mind. It was a big surprise, let me tell you. I haven't heard from her in years. She's here in the valley—has been for over a week, she said. She wanted to know if I would go with her when she goes to find out about claiming the body."

Anna nodded. "I'd hate to be alone at a time like that. The poor woman will need some support."

The others agreed.

"Maybe you can bring her to the Quilting Bee sometime," Clare suggested.

"Oh, yes," Anna agreed. "Wouldn't it be nice to meet Jonathan Hunter's mother?"

"Does she quilt?" the more practical Louise wanted to know.

"I really don't know." Maggie thought they were probably attributing more to her friendship with Carmen than was really there. "I think she sewed. We weren't close; I knew her as a neighbor and the mother of Michael's friend. She was a quiet woman and rather shy. I was surprised to hear from her last night. In fact, I'm surprised she didn't try to call Michael instead. She did say she thought of it but wouldn't have felt right appealing to him. Since she hadn't seen him since he was a child, you know."

"Did Michael say anything about what happened to Jonathan's car?" Louise asked. "Do they know how he got out there?"

"I asked him about that, but they don't know. The kids party out there on weekends, so there are lots of tire tracks and footprints and things. He mentioned the possibility of a carjacker spotting him driving alone and following him out there."

Edie gave a smug smile.

Maggie's hand stilled on the quilt top. "Oh, I almost forgot the most important thing he told me last night. He got a call from Hal. It seems Jon was out there a week ago looking at the property Hal has on the market. He told him not to tell us about it—he wanted to surprise Michael or something."

"Oh, my," Victoria said. "He might have gone out to look at the property."

"Or taken someone out to look at it," Louise said.

"My thought exactly," Maggie admitted. "But Michael says that if he did, no one is saying. He thinks if that was the case it must have been one of the other actors."

"Or maybe a crazed fan," Clare suggested.

Edie and Anna looked at her in surprise. Victoria stopped her stitching for a moment to think this over.

"I guess I assumed the body was dumped there," Victoria said, resuming her stitching with barely a pause.

"If he'd driven out, wouldn't the police have found the car, and wouldn't the reporters have found out?" Louise questioned.

"Those reporters are so nosy and so pushy nowadays," Edie announced, forcing Maggie to fake a cough to cover an incredulous snort. Edie could be describing herself.

Louise threw Maggie a sympathetic look. She was muffling a cough of her own. "A car would be pretty noticeable out in the desert there, even if it was parked a ways from where the body was found."

Maggie nodded her agreement. "I saw the area where the body was found yesterday when I was out riding."

This information was greeted with a rush of comments and questions from the others. It took a few minutes before Maggie was able to continue.

"It's there in the foothills, nowhere near any homes. A car would be easily visible. Especially from the air. And all the TV stations had their helicopters out there on Monday. They'd have seen it and reported it to the police. And all of us," she added.

There was a moment of silence while they all thought about this. Maggie was pressed to provide a detailed description of the crime scene. The others listened, fascinated. They continued to discuss the murder for the rest of the morning, but were unable to come to any conclusions.

Chapter Six

Maggie drove to the Gammage that evening, though Victoria offered, thinking her friend might still be upset about Jon's sudden death. Weeks ago, they had signed up to work this Tuesday evening and Maggie insisted that she still wanted to go. As they drove to the theater, Maggie and Victoria discussed the phone call from Carmen.

"I could hardly believe it," Maggie said. "We lost touch so many years ago, and then to hear from her like that."

"I think that she needs someone strong to lean on. And she remembered you."

Maggie shook her head in wonder.

"Well, you certainly had a few things to tell the others this morning. I don't know how you'll be able to top what you learned yesterday."

But they knew that the others would be anxiously awaiting their "report" of the atmosphere at the theater this evening. After all, tonight would be the first performance since Jonathan's death, Monday being the performers' night off. Anna had commented that they should close the performance out of respect for the deceased, but Louise had pointed out that that would hardly be fair to the thousands of people who held tickets for the evening. Victoria had acknowledged that the theater held almost three thousand people and the *Phantom* performances were all supposed to be sold out. Clare was especially interested in hearing about the actors, and wanted Maggie and Victoria to "check out" the man who replaced Jon.

"Do you think Jon's death could have something to do with the play?" Victoria asked. Clare's comments about books where understudies killed the lead actors continued to interest the women of the Bee. Clare herself was so taken by this theory, she had gone to the library on Monday evening and looked for the books that used the premise. She promised to reread the books and review the plots with the others.

Maggie turned into the parking lot, almost empty now, an hour and a half before the start of the show. "I don't see how. But at this point anything is possible. If we can believe the television and newspaper accounts, the police have no leads at all."

"Maybe the police are just keeping things quiet. Don't they sometimes have important clues that they don't reveal to the public? At least until they finish their investigation?"

Maggie shrugged. "Maybe. I hope so." She maneuvered the car into a parking space and turned off the engine. "Anyway, I think we should go to the stage door tonight and try to meet some of the actors. Then we could ask them about Jonathan ourselves."

Victoria seemed dubious, but she did admit that the others would certainly like to hear about their meeting any of the actors. Before getting out of the car, they agreed to meet at the stage door after the show.

As they climbed the steps at the box office entrance, they joined two other volunteers. Greetings were exchanged, along with murmurings about the horror of Jonathan Hunter's death.

Jonathan's death remained the prime topic of conversation in the lobby where the volunteers joined the floor managers already at work at the long tables set up there. Talk moved as quickly as hands while they stuffed the programs for the evening's performance. Any changes in the cast had to be amended by papers inserted into the preprinted program. Obviously, they would be stuffing programs for the remainder of the performances unless new programs were printed.

Maggie noticed that Victoria's guess had been correct. Jeff Manchester, the man who usually played André, was taking the part of the Phantom. Other slips of paper indicated that the part of André would be played by Kevin Czar and Carlotta would be played by Judith Noonan. It took time to gather the slips of paper, one for each change, and insert them into each of the three thousand programs needed for the evening's performance.

"It must be awfully hard for Tanya," Letitia, one of the floor managers, commented, mentioning the name of the actress who usually played Carlotta. "They were dating, you know."

There were a few murmurs of agreement around the table, along with comments from those who were hearing of it for the first time.

"I heard that the police think she did it," a thin young man with glasses said.

"It's usually the girlfriend—or the wife," Dominic commented. Beside him, his wife nodded. Both of them were retired police officers.

"Do you think she's not here because she's been arrested?" someone asked.

"I guess we'll find out on the late news."

Unable to see the last two speakers, Maggie wondered who made the final remark. Unless they left after the intermission, no one would be home early enough to watch the 10:00 news.

Before more could be said, the programs were gathered up and the pre-performance meeting began. Maggie was glad to hear she'd been assigned a door near the stage on the back side. In her opinion, it offered the best view of the show for the volunteers, who usually had to watch from the aisles. And tonight she wanted to watch the show, to get the actors straight in her mind. Victoria was upstairs on the first balcony, also a good location. Maggie hoped she, too, would take this opportunity to observe the actors.

Maggie enjoyed the time before the show. The patrons came in, took the program she offered, then wandered through the lobby. They often stopped to talk, telling of previous performances they'd seen of *Phantom of the Opera*. There was an air of happy anticipation. Tonight, however, everyone wanted to ask the ushers' opinion of the murder. Had she met Jonathan Hunter? What was he like? Maggie was exhausted by the time the house was opened and she escaped the crowded lobby for her spot at the inside door. Here, the patrons entered in smaller groups, so she was no longer faced with a large crowd asking questions to which she had no answers.

Before long, the tones sounded, the lights dimmed, and the auction on stage began. There was a "hold" at the start of the show, so no one could enter the theater for the first seven to ten minutes. Maggie leaned back against the door frame, braced herself for the explosion at the end of the auction scene, then lost herself in the opening strains of Andrew Lloyd Webber's overture. Halfway through the overture, there would be a rush as the latecomers entered. There were few empty seats in her area, except for four places near the center of row seven. Maggie expected such excellent seats would be filled by then.

Maggie had hoped that the magic of the music would make her forget—take her out of this dismal mood she'd been in the last few days. The memories tinged with sadness seemed to stem from the news of Hal's decision to sell the old ranch land. The news about Jonathan had just made things worse.

But instead of being lost in the music, Maggie felt herself dwelling on Jonathan. He was all she could think about as the show progressed and the Phantom began to appear. Jeff Manchester was good. All the actors were good. She had enjoyed the show tremendously the last time and thought it very well done. And now again, with so many different actors performing the leading roles, it was once again wonderful. But as Jeff's voice soared upward in the beautiful notes of "Music of the Night," Maggie realized that Jonathan had been better. Perhaps it was just her own personal prejudice, but Jonathan's voice had raised goose bumps on her skin with its sheer beauty. More and more it made her think of the waste, this loss of a young man in the prime of his life. What could possibly justify it?

Finally, the chandelier crashed and the lights came up. Maggie pulled herself from the doldrums and went back to work.

During the intermission, several people stopped to ask for directions to the restroom. Business as usual. But several other patrons stopped to ask if she'd seen Jonathan Hunter perform. And how was the new Phantom in relation to him?

Maggie suppressed her true opinion. Who was she to spoil someone's evening?

"He's just as good. They're all wonderful."

After the show, for the first time since they had started volunteering, Maggie and Victoria went to the stage door to await the exodus of the performers. They usually, like many other volunteers, rushed out during the curtain call so they could beat the traffic. But tonight Maggie wanted to play the ardent fan and wait for the actors to exit.

"What do you think we might learn?" Victoria asked.

"I don't know," Maggie admitted. "Nothing probably, but you never know what you might overhear. I would like to meet some of the people Jonathan worked with, though. Just to see what they're like. And the traffic will thin out while we wait."

Even before they reached the stage door, they overheard a promising tidbit. Standing behind the hat check, anticipating the mass exodus, one of the assistant house managers was speaking to another. "He was dating Carlotta, you know. That's why she didn't go on tonight. Too upset."

Maggie and Victoria exchanged a look. Someone had mentioned the same thing while they were stuffing programs earlier in the evening.

As it turned out, whether or not they learned anything significant, Maggie and Victoria enjoyed their first experience as stage door Janes. They stood back, behind a group of lively teens seeking autographs for their souvenir programs. Watching the interaction between the actors and their adoring fans was one of the most interesting things Maggie had seen in a long while.

The girls were gushing over a young man with darkly handsome features. His hair fell to his shoulders in thick waves any woman would envy. Maggie recognized him as a dancer from the show. Barely taller than the teens confronting him, he was signing programs and chatting with them, all the while keeping his eye on the woman beside him. Petite and full of nervous energy, she had shoulder-length hair of an undistinguished brown. Next to her companion's, it looked positively mousy. It took Maggie a moment to realize that the young woman was Susanne Koralski, the female lead with the powerful soprano voice.

The teen girls collecting autographs were bombarding the petite actress with questions, not appearing to notice her desire to leave.

Maggie and Victoria smiled at the two actors as they inched away from the teens, who were still congratulating them on a lovely show. The handsome dancer, Roman Maggiore—Maggie learned from a quick peek into her program—smiled and nodded politely toward them. But he had his arm around Susanne as though safeguarding her and they hurried past without stopping. Maggie wondered if she was ill. But she found the young man's protectiveness touching.

Most of the actors and actresses were friendly, happy to hear that they loved the show. Maggie and Victoria greeted many of them, exchanging a sentence or two.

The parking lot was almost empty when a tall redhead with a long face exited the building. She still wore heavy eye makeup and her short auburn hair was damp and straggly. The teen girls were busy with the actress who played Meg, so the redhead slipped by them unnoticed until Maggie hurriedly approached her.

"You played Carlotta, didn't you?" At her smile and nod, Maggie continued. "I love this play and you were wonderful. You have a marvelous voice."

"Why, thank you." Judy Noonan offered a wide, genuine smile.

"We're volunteer ushers here," Maggie said, indicating Victoria beside her, "and we never tire of seeing the show. We saw it last week with Jonathan Hunter. It's so interesting to see it again tonight with so many of the actors playing different parts."

Maggie paused, wondering just how to phrase what she wanted to say. Nothing wonderfully diplomatic occurred to her, so she just plunged in. "I heard that the actress who usually plays Carlotta was very distressed over the death of Jonathan Hunter. I knew him when he lived here years ago, you know. He and my son were friends."

Judy had arched a brow at Maggie's comment about her friend but now her face turned serious. "Really? Jonathan Hunter lived in Phoenix?"

"In Scottsdale. Years and years ago when he and my Michael were boys. In third grade they had the same teacher. Fifth, too. He and Michael were very good friends." Maggie's voice softened. "He was such a sweet child."

Maggie saw a look she couldn't define in the woman's eyes. "Yeah, he was a sweet man, too. Jonathan Hunter, nice guy. It's been hard for all of us tonight."

Maggie stared at her. Although her tone was conversational and sincere, her words seemed tinged with sarcasm. Maggie thought she was a more complex person than she was letting on. "Will you do Carlotta tomorrow night, too?"

The woman nodded. “All week, I think. Unless Tanya can pull herself together sooner. She and Jon were pretty serious.”

“I had no idea.”

“Had you seen him then, since the run started?”

“Jonathan?” Maggie shook her head. “No. Sorry to say we were all coming to see the show together this week. All my family, that is. Jon had given my son Michael tickets for all of us for this Friday. They kept in touch over the years.” Maggie shook her head. “I really regret not stopping here after the show last week. I would have liked to see him again, to tell him how good I thought he was.”

“He would have liked that.”

Did she detect a hardness to Judy’s tone that seemed out of place with everything else she’d told her? Maggie gave herself an internal shake. Already, her tentative venture into detective work was making her cynical and suspicious.

Sudden screeches from the teenage girls still standing near the door had the three women turning. At the moment, the girls were doing more jumping and bouncing than standing. A rather tall actor with mussed blond hair had just stepped outside and stood in their midst. He had a youthful face with classically handsome features. The three women watched as he greeted the enthusiastic group with a devastating smile.

“That’s Jeff Manchester,” Judy told Maggie and Victoria. “He played the Phantom tonight.”

“He was marvelous,” Victoria declared.

Judy smiled, a wide, genuine smile that lit her eyes. “Yes, Jeff is good. He’s very nice, too.”

“Like Jonathan?” Maggie had to ask. Judy had said the same thing about Jonathan after all, yet somehow she sounded more enthusiastic in her praise of Jeff.

“Ah, yes. Of course.” Judy looked over to the younger actor, who was waving good-bye to the teens as they were being urged toward the parking lot by a parent. He glanced over at the same moment.

"Judy. You're still here. Want a ride?"

Judy greeted him with pleasure, introducing him to Maggie. "This is tonight's Phantom . . . Jeff Manchester." Judy squinted at Maggie's name tag. "Maggie knew Jonathan when he was a kid. He was a friend of her son's."

Some unspoken communication seemed to pass between them before he turned to greet Maggie and Victoria. But as he spoke a few words to them, Maggie decided she must be nursing an overactive imagination. Judy and Jeff were most likely dating, and simply communicating with each other through their eyes. She and her Harry had been able to do that—just a quick look and they'd known what the other was thinking.

When Maggie pulled herself back into the present, Victoria was complimenting Jeff on his singing voice.

"Yes, you were marvelous," Maggie agreed. "It must have been exciting for you, playing the lead. Do you get to do it often?"

"Fairly often, actually. Jon was very careful of his voice and took off anytime he had a sore throat."

"Did you get on with him?"

If Jeff thought her questions were nosy and intrusive, he didn't let on. Except for a quick flash of something in his eyes, he didn't look surprised or offended at her rude question. Polite and gracious, he answered her as though she had every right to interrogate him.

"Sure, we got along. He was okay."

After a few more words about the quality of the performance, they parted with friendly smiles, Maggie and Victoria heading for the nearly deserted parking lot. Jeff led Judy to his car parked in a prime location near the stage door.

Maggie looked back after she unlocked the car door, frowning as she watched the nondescript sedan pull out of its space and start down the drive. Victoria looked across the roof of the car toward her, waiting patiently for her friend to unlock the passenger side door.

"I wonder if Jonathan parked there?" Maggie's voice was low, the question rhetorical. But a young man, one of the assistant floor managers who was getting into his own car beside theirs, answered her.

"Yeah, he did. The star usually gets that space."

Maggie, suddenly brightly alert, turned toward the young man. She thought his name was Ted, but wasn't certain, so she didn't address him by name. "Do you know what kind of car Jonathan Hunter had?"

"Yeah, sure." Ted's eyes lit up. "He had this way cool Bravada."

Maggie had no idea what model that was and it must have shown on her face. Ted elaborated.

"It's a sport utility vehicle, from Oldsmobile. A lot more upscale than the Blazer or the Jimmy. Boy, would I like a car like that."

Maggie saw his eyes move over to his own car, a beat-up Chevy at least ten years old. His tone was wistful as he continued to describe Jon Hunter's car.

"All-wheel-drive, metallic green paint job. California plates that said Phantom, only spelled PHNTM." He shook his head. "A totally cool car. I wonder what happened to it?"

"I was just wondering the same thing," Maggie said, wishing Ted good night.

"That sounds like the kind of car someone might want to steal," Victoria stated thoughtfully once they were seated in Maggie's car.

"I was thinking the same thing." Maggie inserted the key into the ignition. The motor turned over, settling into a low, smooth hum while she latched her seat belt. "Ted certainly was impressed by it. It puts a whole new spin on this, doesn't it?"

"What do you mean?"

"Well . . ." Maggie backed out of her space, and headed toward the exit. "Talking to Judy and Jeff I couldn't help thinking that they were hiding something. Lying about him maybe. But after hearing what Ted had to say about the car I'm wondering if he was carjacked. A carjacker might kill someone and dump the body." Maggie remained silent while she negotiated the turns that would take them back out to Apache Boulevard. When she was finally heading for Rural she continued. "And if it was a carjacking, the person doing it could have picked up the car almost anywhere."

"Oh, my." Victoria realized immediately what that meant.

"Yes," Maggie agreed with her unspoken words. "It means we don't know anything at all. Because it could have happened anywhere."

Chapter Seven

Victoria picked Maggie up the following morning. The women were tired after their late night at the theater and made the short trip in silence.

It was a beautiful spring day and they entered the church courtyard to find that the other Bee members had moved the frames outdoors and were stitching beneath the spreading branches of an old olive tree. Birds sang. The water in the central fountain cascaded downward with a soothing sound. A faint floral fragrance drifted on the air from the first of the blooming decorative orange trees.

By the time Maggie picked up her needle, the peace of the outdoor setting had infected her spirit. She felt better than she had since first hearing about Jonathan, and she was eager to share the news of her visit with the actors the previous evening.

Clare was more than eager to hear about it. She waited impatiently for Maggie and Victoria to settle themselves before asking about the show. "So how was the show without Jonathan?"

"Oh, it was very good," Victoria replied. "It's such a wonderful show and all the actors have such beautiful voices."

"Yes, it was as good as ever," Maggie agreed. "Though, really, I did prefer Jonathan in the part."

The others nodded, accepting the fact that Maggie would be partial to the actor she had once known.

"Well, of course," Anna replied. "He was like a son to you, after all."

Maggie's head went up in surprise. She hadn't ever phrased her relationship to Jon in those terms, but it was true. He'd been there among her own young sons, and she had treated him as one of them. That must be why his death had so affected her.

Maggie was still examining this new insight when Victoria spoke.

"Maggie and I stopped after the show to meet some of the actors."

"Oh, how exciting." So exciting, Clare stuck her finger and had to stop her stitching while she checked for blood. No one wanted blood stains on the quilt. "I wish I'd been there. What were they like? Did you meet the understudy?"

Louise laughed at Clare's rush of questions, but Maggie could see that everyone was interested in the answers.

"Actually, we did meet the understudy who went on last night. Jeff Manchester."

"A very nice young man," Victoria said. "Good-looking, too."

"I thought we should meet some of them in person," Maggie went on. "And it was interesting. They kind of trickle out after the show, coming out the stage door in twos and threes. The orchestra members, too. There were some teenage girls there, collecting autographs and screaming over everyone."

Victoria nodded. "It was quite an experience, I have to admit. I've been to many shows in my lifetime, but I've never waited to meet an actor before. I had no idea so many people did."

"I don't know what you'll be learning from them," Edie commented. "They're actors after all. They lie for a living."

Louise frowned at Edie. "I don't think you can call acting 'lying' for a living."

"What else do you call it? Grown people pretending to be someone they're not. Adults pretending to be children or teenagers. Bimbos playing serious roles."

Victoria seemed startled at her logic, but Maggie and Louise laughed. Edie had always refused to watch television shows where twentysomething actors portrayed high school kids.

Clare refused to let her excitement be dampened by Edie. "What did you say to them?"

Maggie and Victoria reproduced the conversations as best as they could. Clare, whose finger had not bled after all, stitched with only half her attention while she listened carefully. "And what was your impression of them? Especially Jeff."

Maggie had to give Clare credit. That was certainly the important question here.

"There was something about the way they looked at each other when they talked about Jonathan." Maggie glanced at Victoria. "Victoria didn't notice it, but I thought it was strange. Like they had secrets they were being careful to keep. At first I thought Judy was being sarcastic in her comments about Jonathan. But she still seemed sincere."

"Humph." Edie had already voiced her opinion on *that* subject.

"And even though Jeff was very polite, I thought I saw a quick flash of anger—or something—when I asked what he really thought of Jonathan."

"Of course it was a fairly rude question," Louise commented. "He had every right to be angry."

"That's what was strange," Maggie replied. "It was just this quick look in his eyes. I mean, he could have told me to mind my own business. But he didn't. Except for that one moment, he was the nice, polite friend of the deceased."

The others puzzled over this for a moment.

"Tell them about the car," Victoria urged.

"Did you find out what happened to his car?" Louise looked up from the rose she was quilting into the upper corner of the fan block. "I still think that's the key."

"We learned from one of the floor managers that Jonathan had a very nice sport utility vehicle. A Bravada, he called it. It was obvious he thought it was a wonderful car." Maggie cut her thread but didn't start a new one.

Victoria smiled. "He said it was 'way cool.' "

But Maggie wouldn't be distracted by the young man's slang. "I think learning about the kind of car he had makes me wonder if this case will ever be solved. That's just the kind of car that would appeal to a young man out on the streets at that hour and up to no good. A couple of kids in a car could have followed Jonathan out to North Scottsdale, waited until he stopped, and then stolen his car. And in that case, he might have stopped there where he was found, or not."

Edie was nodding in smug agreement, but Clare moaned. "Oh, dear. The more we learn, the more confused I get."

"We did hear one interesting bit of gossip," Maggie said. "Apparently Jon and Tanya Kessler, one of the actresses, were dating."

"Oh, that wasn't gossip, Maggie." Victoria's voice was soft but definite. "Judy confirmed it, remember? She said they were 'serious,' I believe."

Maggie nodded. "And one of the students seemed to think the police suspected her of killing him."

"It's usually the spouse, or the girlfriend or boyfriend," Louise agreed.

Anna sighed. "Clare is right. It's all very confusing. And it would have been so exciting to work this out on our own."

"Well, I for one am ready for a break," Maggie declared, pinning her needle into the quilt top and getting to her feet. She stretched her back for a moment. "Anyone else want some coffee or tea?"

Louise and Victoria stood as well, Anna following more slowly. Then Edie.

By the time they returned with their mugs in hand, their minds were no longer on Jonathan Hunter. Edie was finishing a lengthy explanation of how to piece stars with a particular type of ruler she had just gotten.

As they settled at the frame once more, Louise asked Maggie what she was working on at the moment. The women quilted each morning at the church, but it was understood that they all spent many more hours at home working on blocks and putting together tops. Many of these tops found their way to the church to be quilted for the auction at the bazaar. Others were made for family members, or just for the fun of it.

"I was thinking of starting some blocks in a rose pattern," Maggie told her friends. The rose was a popular pattern among the Bee women; there were dozens of variations and they felt it especially appropriate to the St. Rose Quilting Bee. "I've been reminiscing a lot lately." Maggie sighed. "I used to have a rose garden at the back of the house. Actually, it's still there; Sara looks after it."

Maggie paused, remembering the rose garden. She didn't mention it to the others, but the reason she especially wanted to do a rose quilt had something to do with the voice she still heard singing in her head. Jon had always loved the roses she grew along the back of the house. She tended them while the boys played in the backyard, so the smell of roses always took her back to those early years when she did her gardening and the boys played on their swings and in the sandbox Harry had built for them. Jon had been there as often as not, playing with her boys. Maggie wondered if she could work through some of her unsettled feelings by creating a quilt of roses. She shook her head, trying to clear it of some of the memories.

"I've been thinking about the days when the boys were little and I tended my rose garden while they played. The smell of roses always takes me back to that time. I was thinking of doing some rose blocks. The pink-and-yellow blooms were always my favorites—you know the ones. They're yellow, but the edges of the blossoms are pink. So

I thought of using pinks and yellows for the roses. Wouldn't that make for some pretty blocks?"

Victoria admitted that it would. "Perhaps some peach as well," she suggested.

Maggie liked the sound of peach fabric roses mingling with the yellow and pink. Pictures of quilt patterns flashed through her mind as she considered what design she might use.

"If you need some fabric, I have a solid in a lovely shade of peach. Some salmon pink, too," Anna offered.

Maggie thanked her distractedly. Her mind was still taken up by thoughts of the new quilt. There was a rose wreath she had seen on an old quilt. . . .

The others smiled at one another across the quilt frame. They understood that excitement that came with the first inspiration. They spoke around her of other things—of quilts they were planning for the Bee auction, of tops they hoped to finish for themselves or for members of their families.

The others would have been surprised to learn that Maggie's continued distraction had nothing to do with her creation of the rose quilt. The excitement over the new design had flown when a new thought popped into her head. It came out of nowhere, but quickly grabbed her full attention. While her fingers continued to stitch along the light pencil lines that delineated the rose-bedecked fan she was quilting into one of the alternate blocks, her mind was busy dissecting this new idea.

Jonathan's car was still missing, supposedly stolen the night of his death. The police were apparently working on the theory that he was killed by carjackers who followed him and took advantage of his being alone in a deserted location. But Jonathan had spent the hours before his death having a late supper with other members of the cast. What if he'd brought a friend from the cast out to see the land he was hoping to buy? Michael said none of them admitted to accompanying him. But, as Edie had reminded them, they *were* actors.

Maggie's eyes brightened as she pondered who might have gone with him, who might have had reason to want him dead, who had the physical ability to move him out of the car after the fact. There was Tanya, the young woman he'd been dating. But a woman might not be strong enough to lift a man, especially a dead one, out of a vehicle.

Her hands stilled on the quilt top. Why was she thinking that he had to be moved out of the car? Wouldn't it be perfectly natural for someone to drive to a piece of property, then get out of the car with a friend to look over the land?

Maggie's hands began to move again, her practiced fingers pushing the needle in and out of the fabric with a quick, steady rhythm. Of course this theory had its own problems. It would have been dark, though there had been a partial moon that night. What could he have shown to a friend on a dark night? And Jonathan's body was found several hundred feet away from the property Hal was offering for sale. If he had a four-wheel-drive vehicle, why didn't he drive right up to the parcel itself?

The conversation over quilt patterns continued to swirl around her. Maggie retained enough consciousness of what was being said to make a comment now and then, but the main part of her brain continued to work over the question of Jonathan Hunter and what he was doing the night of his death. She needed to meet Tanya. When would that young woman return to the performance?

Clare was describing a family reunion quilt she was organizing for their big family get-together that summer. She'd washed and cut all the fabric and was now sending it out to the various family members to inscribe.

"So many of the younger people don't sew at all," she lamented. "I said I would stitch the blocks for those who couldn't, but I had no idea there would be so many."

"Doesn't surprise me at all," Edie commented. "All they do is watch TV."

"A memory quilt!"

Maggie's exclamation dropped into the brief silence that followed Edie's remark. Clare turned a strange look her way.

"I told you about the reunion quilt last fall," Clare reminded Maggie. "You helped me decide on a pattern."

"Oh, yes, I remember." Maggie's voice was distracted. "That isn't what I meant. I was just thinking of memory quits—ones you make in memory of a person. Kind of like the mourning quilts they used to make in Victorian times."

Victoria raised an eyebrow as her eyes met Maggie's across the frame. A smile tilted one corner of her lips. Maggie returned it.

"Victoria knows what I'm thinking."

"But I don't know where you're heading with it."

"Well, do please enlighten the rest of us," Louise urged. "Are you thinking of making a quilt in memory of Jonathan Hunter?"

"Oh, what a wonderful idea!" Clare was instantly supportive.

"If all of you will help, we could make the blocks and then have the cast members sign them. We could give it to Carmen."

Anna was the first to agree. "What a nice thing to do for your old friend. Of course I'll help."

The others quickly added their support. Even Edie.

"But how will you get them signed by the cast?" Clare was anxious to help but she didn't know how Maggie would accomplish this most important step.

"That will be the tricky part," Maggie decided. "What do you say we call the theater, Victoria, and see if they need any ushers tonight or tomorrow?"

Chapter Eight

When Maggie returned home from St. Rose that afternoon, she was looking forward to a quick lunch and a long nap. The late night at the theater on Tuesday, another restless night of indistinct but troubling dreams, and the mental strain of trying to provide all the possible scenarios of what might have happened early Monday morning had left her exhausted.

But she'd been home a mere fifteen minutes when the doorbell rang. Before she had a chance to get even halfway there from the kitchen, the bell rang again. And yet again, as she approached the door.

Wondering who might be out there and so anxious to have an answer to the bell's summons, Maggie hesitated. The condominium complex had a no soliciting rule, but people sometimes tried to sell door-to-door anyway. As the bell rang once more, Maggie checked the peephole. A middle-aged woman stood there, her finger poised over the bell, ready to ring it again. Maggie flung the door open.

"Oh, Maggie, thank goodness. I thought you weren't here."

Maggie would have known her anywhere. About five-feet-four, a little heavier than she had once been. Her hair was as thick and black as ever, though Maggie thought it was probably out of a bottle these days. She was still attractive, but her olive complexion looked splotchy and her eyelids were drooping and puffy.

"I only just got back," Maggie said, watching as Carmen Hunter bustled past her into the house. "I quilt at the church every morning."

"Oh, that's just the kind of thing you would do," Carmen said, leading Maggie to speculate over just what she meant by the comment.

"Has something happened?" Maggie wondered what else could possibly happen after your son was murdered, but there had to be some reason why Carmen was here, leaning on her doorbell. A thought suddenly occurred to her. "Did the police make an arrest?"

"Oh, how I wish they had." Carmen held her hand to her mouth, a crumpled tissue held tight. A muffled sob escaped. "Then they would stop harassing me . . ."

Maggie led her into the kitchen, steering her to a seat at the table. She sat beside her. "What do you mean, 'harassing' you?"

Maggie was tired and hungry and in no mood for guessing games. But then she took a closer look at Carmen and all her resentment fled. Carmen had always been a pretty woman, one who took great care with her appearance. Earlier, at the door, she'd been so surprised to see Carmen and to realize how easily she recognized her, that specifics had not registered.

Now, she examined the woman sitting beside her. Her splotchy face and puffy lids told of recently shed tears. Since her son had just been murdered, Maggie did not find that unusual. But she now noticed for the first time her creased and rumpled dress, her messed hair. The Carmen she had known would not have gone out in public that way. Her hair had always been perfectly arranged, her clothes neat and pressed.

Maggie couldn't turn away from someone in such distress. Imagine if it had been Michael who had been found out there in the desert. Then she would be the one needing support from friends.

Quickly, Maggie rose from the table. "Let me put on some tea."

"Oh, Maggie, you're so sweet."

Maggie left Carmen to sit while she got out the cups and tea bags. By the time the water was hot and she poured out the tea, Carmen had composed herself.

"Now, tell me what happened that has you so agitated."

Carmen started right in. "Remember when I called? I asked if you would go to the police station with me—to see about having the body released. Well, this morning the detective in charge of the case came over to my apartment. He had told me he wanted to talk to me again, but I just thought we would go over to the police station and do it. The two of us together." She smiled weakly at Maggie. "I thought I might need a little moral support."

Maggie didn't know what to say.

"I wish you had been there with me this morning." Carmen took a sip of her tea, but it did nothing to calm her agitation. "Oh, Maggie, it was horrible. He asked me all kinds of questions. About how Jon and I got along. And where I was that night. It's like he thinks I killed my own son." Carmen stopped talking as she burst into tears.

Surprised and wondering what spin Carmen might be putting on her experience with the detective, Maggie tried to reassure her.

"I'm sure they have to ask everybody where they were. It's probably all routine. It's the kind of thing he'll need to know to find out who did it."

Carmen continued to sob. "It was horrible. Awful."

Maggie sat at the table beside her, at a loss. Carmen was rapidly working herself into hysteria. Finally, Maggie stood and took her by the arm.

"Why don't I just show you where the bathroom is and you can get yourself calmed down and put back together." To her relief, Carmen didn't resist, just let Maggie lead her down the hall. "I haven't had my lunch yet, and I'm getting hungry. I'll put on some soup," she added.

They had reached the bathroom by now, and Maggie helped Carmen inside. She put her handbag on the counter and took a new washcloth and towel from the cupboard. Then she closed the door, telling Carmen to come back to the kitchen when she was done.

Maggie returned to the kitchen to defrost and heat up some homemade split pea soup. The soup was almost ready, a pan of biscuits were in the oven, and she was setting the table when she heard Carmen reenter the room.

"I always like a bowl of soup, even if my appetite is down," Maggie began. Then she looked up and saw her guest and lost her train of thought.

Carmen had freshened up in a big way. And to think she had been worrying about her, Maggie thought, laughing inwardly at herself. Here she'd been imagining poor Carmen in the bathroom, sobbing her heart out over her murdered son. She'd even debated going in and calling through the door, to reassure her.

But now here she was. And Carmen looked wonderful. Her dress was still a bit wrinkled, but her hair was perfectly combed. Her eyes were bloodshot, but she'd applied makeup with a skillful touch that Maggie envied. Carmen was over fifty but you'd never know it to look at her.

"I feel so much better now," Carmen told her. "And you're right. A bowl of soup is always nice."

Still blinking at the change in her guest, Maggie gave a startled jump when the oven buzzer sounded. Within minutes, the biscuits were on the table, the soup ladled into bowls, and iced tea poured into tall glasses.

"This is so nice of you, Maggie," Carmen said as she sat down at the table.

"It's no trouble," Maggie assured her. She opened a napkin over her lap. "The years have certainly treated you kindly, Carmen."

"You're very sweet, Maggie, to say that." Carmen put down her spoon and tapped the corner of her mouth with her napkin.

"Well, it's the truth. You must have done very well out in California."

"It was a struggle for a while. But I couldn't stay out here after Ed disappeared." She gave a short, mirthless laugh. "Disappeared. That was the polite way to say that he ran out on us. I was so embarrassed. I couldn't stay, knowing that everyone was talking about it, saying that my husband left and didn't even say good-bye."

"Oh, Carmen, I'm sure that wasn't the case."

"It's nice of you to say so, Maggie, but I know it was." Carmen's voice took on a hard edge. The soft vulnerability she'd always worn, and that Maggie had detected in her voice over the phone, was gone. "I had family in Los Angeles, so it was a good move for us. Though Jon did have trouble settling in at school. But I got a job in a nursing home and started taking classes to finish up my nursing degree. There I could pretend that I was a widow, so that everyone wouldn't feel sorry for me because my husband deserted us."

Maggie hardly knew what to say. She murmured something she hoped was appropriate and busied herself buttering a biscuit. Carmen was certainly proving to be an enigma. Maggie was beginning to realize that she didn't know the woman at all. And the idea Carmen had dropped earlier, that she might be a suspect, had Maggie's mind in a turmoil. Maggie decided to talk about the old days. "Have you seen any of the other people from the old neighborhood? A lot of them still live out there, you know."

"No," Carmen replied. "I didn't keep up much. You should know that. I would have stayed in touch with you, if anyone."

Maggie tried not to show her surprise. She had never considered Carmen a close friend. It was the boys who were close. Though she'd liked Carmen, she was just the mother of Michael's friend, a casual acquaintance.

"I did see that Winona Winthrop on TV. I guess she must have enjoyed that . . . finding the body. She always was a busybody."

"Oh, I don't know . . ." Maggie began.

Carmen's voice took on a note of comradely goodwill. "Oh, come now. Don't you remember how she was at the neighborhood get-togethers? Always asking personal questions—what are you doing and what is Ed doing? And how about that little boy of yours?"

Maggie did remember Winona. But her memories differed from Carmen's. Winona's husband had died quite suddenly while still young. She'd been left alone with the ranch to look after and no family—just an aging cocker spaniel. She certainly did ask the kind of questions Carmen mentioned. But Maggie felt she had a sincere interest in what the others were doing. Winona led a lonely life; Maggie couldn't begrudge her the pleasure of sharing in her own family's activities if only in a vicarious way.

Shaking her head over how differently two people can remember the same person, Maggie was relieved when Carmen asked her to pass the pepper. It was the perfect time to change the subject.

"So . . . have you been in the valley long?"

Carmen's appetite was much better than Maggie had expected. She was eating the homemade soup with enthusiasm and had already finished two biscuits. She reached for a third before answering.

"I came just before the cast arrived. A realtor I know in Los Angeles helps me find inexpensive places to stay so that I can watch Jon perform. I've seen him in Seattle, Portland, and Denver. Some of the other cities he's been in have been too far away."

"Didn't Jon help you out?" Maggie couldn't help but notice that Carmen spoke of Jon as though he were still alive.

"Oh, no. Half the time he didn't even know I went. He was busy working, and it's important for an actor to concentrate on his role. I didn't want to distract him. He wouldn't have liked that at all."

Carmen took another moment to dab at her mouth. Maggie noted the dark red of her lipstick rubbing off onto the pale paper napkin and was glad she hadn't brought out her good linen ones. Although Carmen spoke with pride of her son and his profession, Maggie wondered if she should revise her opinion of Jon as well. She didn't think Carmen's comments put her son in the best light.

"It's expensive traveling around to see Jon," Carmen continued, "but I don't have a lot of expenses. And the nice thing about doing private-duty nursing is that you can arrange your hours however you want to."

"It's wonderful that you managed to get your degree after you left."

Carmen shrugged. "I'd already done part of the schooling, but when we married Ed wanted me to stay at home." Carmen gave a deep sigh, her chest moving visibly with the effort. "Things were different then."

"They certainly were," Maggie agreed. "All the young women work these days. But it was nice to be able to stay at home with the children, wasn't it? Today's mothers miss a lot of the special moments we had, being there with our sons."

Carmen nodded. "Of course, later I did work part-time at the school." She smiled, her face softening at pleasant memories of the past. "And Jon never seemed to mind that I worked there. He was such a happy little boy."

Maggie smiled, too. "Yes, I remember him very well. How he loved to sing. My boys always asked him if he was going to be a singing cowboy."

Carmen put her spoon down, the last bit of food forgotten. "Oh, he had such a wonderful voice. I always got tears in my eyes to hear him." She used the napkin to dab at her eyes. "I'm getting them now just thinking about it."

"I saw him do the Phantom last week," Maggie admitted. "It's my favorite show. Jon was wonderful in the part. I got shivers down my spine listening to him sing 'Music of the Night.' "

Carmen nodded in agreement. "The move to Los Angeles was probably good for him, careerwise. At first he was miserable, of course. He missed Michael and his other friends. I wanted to send him to a counselor, but it was too expensive. But once he got to middle school, he got involved in the drama department, and then everything was all right."

Maggie got up to refill the tea. The soup had revitalized her; it was comfortable sitting in the cozy kitchen talking. Maggie didn't mind reminiscing about the boys' childhood and she was learning more about both Carmen and Jon.

"I guess they had a good drama program there in the city."

"Oh, my, yes. In no time at all he started auditioning for real parts. He was doing commercials by the time he was fifteen. He wanted to quit school and look for full-time acting work, but I wouldn't let him. He was mad at the time, but he realized it was for the best when he went to UCLA. He didn't graduate, but he had some good parts there and did some television programs. Just bit parts. *Les Miserables* was his big break. He played Enjolras, you know—the revolutionary leader. I was so proud of him. But oh, how I cried when the barricade turned and there he was, dead."

Carmen looked ready to cry now, her eyes tearing almost enough to spill over, so Maggie quickly changed the topic. "It must have been a nice change to see him in this play, where he seems to be immortal."

Carmen looked surprised at this thought, but then a smile tipped her lips and grew into a grin. "Why, that's right isn't it? The chandelier exploding at the beginning and then the disappearance at the end . . ." She paused, thinking, while her eyes sparkled. "It does seem to imply that he's still around after all those years." She sighed. "Immortal. What a lovely thought."

Maggie watched her, glad to have averted more tears. "The other actors all seem to have thought very highly of him."

Carmen gave a short laugh that held little mirth. "Yes, I've been watching the news reports, too. This group has been together for six months. And I've heard a lot about them from Jon." Her tone indicated there was a lot more she could tell Maggie about the group, but she didn't seem anxious to comply.

"I heard he was dating one of the women. Tanya something?"

"Oh, yes. That hussy."

Maggie's eyes widened with surprise. Sweet Carmen had an earthier side.

"I see that look you're giving me, Maggie Browne. But she was. They'd been dating for months but the last time I talked to him, Jon said she'd started flirting like crazy with all the other guys, even the musicians."

"Really?" Maggie didn't know what to say. She had yet to meet Tanya. Now she was more anxious than ever to do so. "She didn't perform last night, you know. Gossip has it that it's because she's so broken up over his death."

Carmen seemed surprised by Maggie's insider knowledge. "You were at the show last night?"

"Why, yes. Didn't I mention it? Victoria and I—she's one of the other women in the Quilting Bee at the church—are volunteer ushers over at the theater. That's how I saw it last week, too, when Jonathan sang."

"Oh, my, you do keep busy, don't you?" Carmen pushed herself up from the table, smoothing down the front of her dress. The gushing friendliness of their earlier reunion was replaced by the polite demeanor of a society matron.

"I really should be going. Thank you so much for everything. The soup was delicious. I haven't made my own soup for years. It's hardly worth it for only one person." As though suddenly realizing that Maggie too lived alone, she hastily amended her earlier statement. "Of course your boys all live here in town, don't they? I expect you have them over quite often."

Maggie was more interested in her original statement about cooking for one. The implication there was what interested her. "I take it Jon didn't get home much."

"No. He was so busy all the time. But he did call to tell me about the run in Phoenix and arranged for tickets. He knew I'd enjoy coming back here."

"But you weren't staying with him?"

Carmen's lips tightened. "No. I expected that hussy he was seeing discouraged that."

Maggie filed away *that* interesting little tidbit. "Do you know where he was staying here in town?"

"Yes. The police told me. A condo in Chandler. I could have taken good care of him there."

They were talking in the hall now, just inside the door. Carmen reached into her purse for a tissue. Maggie was still assimilating the knowledge that the *police* told Carmen where Jon had been living. And she was beginning to think Carmen had been a world-class meddler in her son's life.

Carmen went on. "But the place I'm renting is very nice. I have it for another three weeks."

Maggie didn't make a move to open the door. She was tired and still had much to do today, but this conversation with Carmen was too interesting to abandon. "So Jon was staying in Chandler. But his body was found in the north, completely opposite of where he was staying."

"I think he must have been trying to see some of the old neighborhood," Carmen said. "But I don't know why he would have been there so late at night. It was too late to visit anyone by the time the show let out."

Maggie realized that Carmen didn't know about the land Jon might have been looking at. She ushered her into the living room, urging her to take a seat.

"Carmen, did you know that Jon approached Hal, my oldest son, about buying some land that he has for sale?"

Carmen didn't seem surprised. "The police did say something about that. I didn't know it had anything to do with you and Hal, though." Carmen's fingers pulled at the damp tissue in her hand, causing some of the fibers to shred. "I liked to think that Jon and I were close—and we were," she rushed to add. "But there were a lot of things he didn't tell me. Financial things especially. He was like his father that way."

Maggie felt sorry for Carmen. First to lose her son. And then to have to admit that she didn't know as much about him as she liked to pretend. Maggie wondered how much she really knew about her own sons. She *thought* she knew them very well. But if one of them suddenly died—heaven forbid—would she be surprised by what she learned afterward?

Maggie suddenly remembered one of the Bee members asking if Carmen might like to come to the Quilting Bee. It would be good for Carmen to get out. She needed some distracting activity; she might brood if left alone all day.

"Why don't you come out to St. Rose with us tomorrow, Carmen? Do you quilt?"

Carmen looked surprised, but pleased at the invitation. "I'm afraid I don't," she said. "But how nice of you to ask me. I would like to stop over. Not tomorrow," she added, "but maybe another day."

"You come over anytime." Maggie patted her on the arm. "And I'm sure you can sew. We can teach you how to quilt if you like, or get you started on some other project."

"I used to sew," Carmen admitted. "I used to make all my clothes, back when Jon was a boy. And my mother taught me to embroider. But I haven't for years," she added.

"Well, I'm sure you'll be a natural. We'll set you up with something and you can sit with us and visit. In fact, just today, we were talking about doing a memory quilt for Jonathan. We wondered if the cast would sign blocks for us to put together for you."

Carmen's eyes teared up again. "Oh, Maggie. You are the sweetest person. That is so nice."

"Well, you try to come some morning and join us."

As Maggie escorted Carmen to the door she couldn't resist another question. "Do you think Jon wanted to move back to the old neighborhood?"

Carmen shrugged. It wasn't just a gesture indicating that she didn't know. It was a sign of defeat, an admittance that she no longer knew her son as she wished she did. Maggie realized that her facade had fallen, and the fragile woman beneath was now before her.

"He was very happy there. He always talked about when we lived in Arizona and how wonderful it was. Even when he'd decided he liked L.A., he still called his childhood years here the happiest time of his life."

Maggie nodded absently. But she thought it was sad that a young man of thirty-two should consider his childhood the happiest years of his life. His recent years should have been filled with friends and fun and career highlights. Shouldn't they have been his happiest?

As she reached out to open the front door, Maggie made an offhand remark. "I was out riding the other day and ran into Harley Stoner."

"Oh, my. Harley Stoner." Carmen's voice softened even as her eyes sparkled. "Well, that certainly brings back memories."

Surprised at the effect of her statement on Carmen, Maggie couldn't help but smile. Carmen's reaction was so similar to Harley's. "He remembered you, too."

"Did he?" To Maggie's surprise, a sweet girlish smile lit Carmen's eyes, making her look younger and quite pretty. "He and Ed didn't get along."

"So I gathered."

Carmen looked suddenly flustered. She glanced at her watch and murmured something about the time. With additional thanks to Maggie, she hurried out the door.

Maggie stood a moment, looking after Carmen. Now what was that all about?

Chapter Nine

Maggie's long day wasn't over yet. She called Victoria after Carmen left and learned they were expected at the theater that evening. She changed quickly into her white blouse and black slacks. Victoria insisted on driving, and Maggie was too tired to argue.

During the ride to Tempe, Maggie told Victoria all about her afternoon with Carmen. Victoria agreed that Carmen seemed to be a different woman from the one Maggie had first described. "But after all, Maggie, it has been many years since you knew her. And people change. Especially when things happen like losing your husband. That can harden a person."

Maggie still couldn't quite put her feelings into words. There was something about Carmen but she was unable to grasp it. She remembered a carousel she'd ridden in her youth and the golden ring the children all tried to catch. But it was just tantalizingly out of reach. "Maybe that's all it is. I'm sure I'm not the same person I was twenty years ago."

As they walked into the theater, Victoria asked, "I guess I'll meet you at the stage door again? That is why we came, isn't it? To speak to the actors again?"

Maggie nodded. "Of course. Though I'll enjoy the show as much as always, I'm sure. But I do want to see if I can talk to that nice Judy again. I want to mention the memory quilt to her and see what she says."

So four hours later, Maggie and Victoria were once again standing outside the stage door. There were others there as well, some friends of cast members, some young people looking for autographs.

As the first of the actors began to exit the stage door, the autograph hunters surged forward, all smiles and congratulations. Maggie craned her neck to see who was there. She recognized the two young women greeting their fans as two of the ballet dancers in the show. As they finished signing the proffered programs, the dark young man, Roman, came out, and the young people turned to him with eager smiles. Maggie noted that he was alone, and smiling engagingly at the female members of the group.

Maggie and Victoria nodded and smiled to the various actors and actresses as they passed by them. Susanne Koralski hadn't performed that evening and Tanya Kessler was still out. It took a while before Maggie spotted Judy. She had to wait while the tall redhead signed some programs, but then she approached Maggie and Victoria with a friendly grin.

"Well, hello again. Did you enjoy the show this evening?"

"Always," Maggie responded.

"Oh, yes," Victoria agreed. "You have such a beautiful voice," she added.

While Judy thanked Victoria for the compliment, Maggie formulated in her mind what she would say to her about the memory quilt. As soon as they finished their conversation, Maggie began to speak.

"You know, Judy, in addition to working here, Victoria and I belong to a Seniors' Guild at church where we make quilts."

Judy seemed genuinely interested. "My grandmother used to make quilts," she told them.

Maggie continued. "We were talking about Jonathan today and his mother. I knew her quite well years ago and she's contacted me again recently."

Judy seemed surprised at this information, but didn't say anything. Maggie did notice, however, that her brows drew together. Maggie went on.

"Anyway, we were talking at our Quilting Bee this morning about memory quilts. They're quilts you make in memory of a person after they pass on. And I thought it might be nice to make one for Mrs. Hunter."

Judy smiled a greeting at someone behind Maggie and she turned around to see who was there. Jeff Manchester was pulling away from the young women at the door and coming toward them.

"Jeff," Judy greeted him. "You remember Maggie and Victoria from last night, don't you? They knew Jon when he was a kid." Her voice inched upward at the end of the sentence as though she were asking a question.

"Oh, only Maggie knew him," Victoria corrected.

Jeff acknowledged the correction as he nodded a greeting to the two women. "Sure. How are you tonight?"

"We're well. And you were superb once again." Maggie thought he seemed almost embarrassed at her praise, but he smiled his thanks very nicely. Was there a wary look in his eyes, though? She wished she could have seen his reaction when he first saw they were back.

"Maggie wants to make a special quilt for Jon's mother," Judy told him. "She was just telling me about it."

"Yes. A memory quilt. I was hoping to get your opinion," Maggie told her. "Do you think the company would all sign blocks for such a quilt?"

Judy looked regretful. "It's a great idea. But would we have to know how to sew? I don't know how many people can."

"Oh, you wouldn't have to be able to sew," Maggie assured her. "I would have all the fabric gathered together and cut out. All you'd have to do would be to sign your name—draw a little picture if you feel inclined—that kind of thing. It's almost like an autograph book; you can write little verses and quotations. Only it's all done on fabric."

Judy brightened, a spark of interest lighting her eyes. "What a neat idea. But it doesn't sound like any quilt my grandmother ever made." She looked at Jeff. "What do you think?"

Jeff shrugged. "Sounds okay to me."

"Me, too," Judy agreed.

Maggie smiled. Judy and Jeff made such a nice couple. She didn't know what Carmen was thinking when she implied that the company might not be the pleasant people they seemed to be when interviewed by the media. "Thank you both. Do you think the others would like to participate? I thought maybe I could arrange a barbecue at the ranch on Monday when you all have your day off. Do you think that would work?"

Judy glanced at Jeff, her eyebrows raised. He shrugged. "I know I'd love it," she told Maggie.

"You have a ranch?" Jeff asked.

"Well, I used to. My son has it now, but I think he and his family would enjoy having all of you over." Maggie smiled, sure of her son's compliance. "In fact, we're all coming to the show on Friday night. Jon sent us tickets."

"Jonathan did that?" It was Jeff's turn to raise his eyebrows.

Victoria nodded. "He and Maggie's son were the best of friends."

Maggie saw a particular look pass between the two actors and stepped in to correct what she thought sounded a bit more than the truth. "Well, they were best friends when they were children. But they did keep in touch over the years, in a more casual way." Maggie kept her eyes on the two actors, but whatever she thought she'd seen was gone.

Judy smiled at the two other women. "So you're coming again on Friday. You're going to get tired of the show."

"Oh, never," Victoria exclaimed, and Maggie was quick to echo her.

"But we've got to get going," Maggie said, realizing that the parking lot was virtually empty and that it must be getting very late. "How about if I write up an invitation to bring to you—about the barbecue? Could you pass it around the company, or post it backstage? To see if everyone could come?"

"Sure. If it's real home-cooked food, everyone will come. We don't get that too often on the road. And it's a real nice thing for you to do, Maggie."

"It will be fun," she assured them.

"Well," she told Victoria a few minutes later as they headed back to Scottsdale. "Things are off to a good start. We've made an effort to meet some of Jonathan's coworkers. And Carmen says she'll stop by the Quilting Bee one morning for a visit. If we can learn anything about this, they are the people who should be able to help us."

Victoria seemed skeptical. "I don't see what talking to all these people will do to help catch Jon's killer, though. That's a job for the police, Maggie."

"But it's so interesting to talk to everyone and try to speculate about what happened, don't you think?"

"As an intellectual exercise, perhaps. But don't get so far into it that you put yourself in danger, Maggie."

"Don't be silly." Maggie laughed off Victoria's worries. "What could possibly happen?"

Chapter Ten

Despite her second late night in a row, Maggie was up and heading for Hal's place before sunrise. She'd explained her plan to Victoria on their ride home the night before, asking her not to wait for her that morning; she would head out to St. Rose to join the Quilting Bee after her ride.

Pink and orange were tinting the eastern sky when Maggie guided Chestnut out toward the mountain trail. Thick lavender clouds gathered just over the horizon, dispersing the colors and adding to the beauty of the morning. Maggie found herself forgetting her tiredness as she looked around her. She used to enjoy early-morning rides before moving to her condo; now she rediscovered the joy of it. The sun struggled in its upward journey, creating a soft light, tinted with a peachy glow. Small rabbits were venturing out, holding their little bodies perfectly still to blend into the landscape until Chestnut passed them by.

Maggie took a deep breath, drinking in the unique aroma of nature on a dry desert morning. It was a fresh, clean scent that brought Maggie home, and a peace settled in her that she was more than willing to welcome. She could almost forget that she was on a fact-finding mission and just enjoy the moment for its own sake. Almost.

Maggie knew where Jonathan's body had been found. She knew who had found it. Now she planned to hear the account firsthand from the person who had made the discovery. Winona Winthrop had been interviewed on the news, telling a reporter how awful it was to find a dead body. But unlike Carmen, Maggie did not think Winona enjoyed the experience.

Like Maggie and Harry, Winona and her husband had lived on a small horse ranch. When her husband died, Winona sold off pieces of the property little by little. The ranch was just too much for her to maintain on her own. But she had managed well with the smaller spread, keeping a rental stable and offering riding lessons for many years. Winona still lived on the former Winthrop ranch, now whittled down to the two acres surrounding the main house. She'd made a tidy profit some years ago when she decided to retire and sold the riding stables to a developer.

Maggie supposed she could have called on Winona at her home. But she knew that Winona was a creature of habit. If she had been walking her dog at dawn on Monday morning, then she would be out walking her dog this morning at dawn. And it seemed to Maggie that "bumping into her" in the desert would be just the thing to do in order to casually bring up her Monday morning discovery. Winona knew Maggie used to ride every morning and knew she still liked to come out and ride. She wouldn't think anything of seeing her out on Chestnut. The trick was to discover where she was walking this morning, as Maggie felt sure she would avoid the old trail where the body had been found. At least for now.

Maggie hadn't been riding for long when she spotted a faded yellow sweatshirt up ahead. Five-foot-five, her body whiplash thin and brown as old leather, Winona was striding along, sure-footed as the horse Maggie rode, a black cocker spaniel trotting beside her. Maggie had to smile. If there had been any doubt the woman she saw was Winona, the black cocker erased it. Winona always had a cocker spaniel in the house, almost always a black one—though Maggie thought she remembered a ginger one many years ago, before Winona's husband passed on.

In the early morning quiet, Winona must have heard Chestnut's approach, yet her head remained trained straight ahead and her pace did not slacken. She didn't turn until the cocker ran toward Chestnut and Maggie, barking loudly the whole time.

Maggie called out a greeting, shouting to be heard over the dog.

Winona offered a smile, calling to the dog in a loud, firm voice to be quiet. To Maggie's surprise, the dog obeyed, quieting and trotting back to join his mistress. He sat obediently at her feet, looking up at her with his large dark eyes. Winona remained standing in the spot where she'd stopped when Maggie first greeted her.

As Maggie dismounted and approached, Winona started off walking again, telling Maggie that she wanted to continue her exercise. She'd never even said hello. Maggie wondered if she'd been as blasé with the police after showing them where she'd found the body. *"Well, here it is. I have to continue with my walk now."* Maggie stifled the laughter this thought brought and moved beside her, matching her stride. Chestnut followed obediently behind, led by the reins held in her hand. The cocker ignored them, trotting a few paces ahead, his nose to the ground. Every now and then he looked back to be sure his mistress was still with him.

Although they hadn't seen each other for many months, Winona greeted Maggie as if they'd just visited together last week.

"Watching the place for your son and his wife, I guess."

"I didn't know you knew they were in California." Maggie was surprised. Hal didn't believe in advertising their departures, and rarely told the neighbors when they would be gone. He also refused to cancel the mail or the newspapers, saying the fewer people who knew you were gone the better. Yet this was the second neighbor this week who was aware that Hal and his family were away.

Winona shrugged. "Hal didn't call to tell me, if that's what you mean. But it's pretty obvious they're gone. And I know the school's off this week."

Maggie almost smiled. So much for Hal's theories about discouraging burglars.

"I heard about Jonathan Hunter, of course. It must have been terrible for you," Maggie told Winona.

The other woman loosened up somewhat at this expression of sympathy. "Oh, Maggie, you just don't know. Samson and I were walking along our usual route. It was such a nice morning. And then just over the rise, there was this person, lying there on the ground." Winona's voice shook a little as she remembered. "I thought it must be a homeless person, sleeping out there. Drunk probably. But he wasn't dressed like a homeless person, you know. Just pants and a short-sleeved shirt, the kind the men wear for golf. Those homeless people wear a lot of clothes, and they always seem to have a coat or a sweater on."

Winona stopped to take a breath. Recounting her tale seemed to make her breathless in a way the rapid walking had not.

"Poor Samson got up close and then started barking. He didn't like it at all. And when I got close—I was going to poke him, you know. To wake him up. Well, then I saw the blood on his head." She swallowed. "I just called Samson along and rushed back home and called the police. And then to learn it was that nice Jon Hunter, all grown up." She shook her head. "I talked to my doctor and he wanted to give me tranquilizers. I don't like to take them, but it's so hard to sleep. I keep seeing him lying there—and poor Samson sniffing at the body and barking. And then I wake up and can't get back to sleep." Winona shuddered. "In all the years I've been walking Samson on that trail, we've never seen so much as a dead rabbit."

Maggie put her arm around Winona's shoulders. Sometimes physical contact with another human was better than any words. Maggie was surprised that Winona was taking it so hard. She'd always seemed such a strong, practical person, up to facing anything that could arise. But she did dote on her dog.

"And how is Samson?"

"He's been traumatized." Her voice rose on the last word, drawing it out for emphasis with her hand gripped tightly on Maggie's arm. "I've had to change our morning walk route and that's added to the problem. He doesn't like any change in his routine." Winona looked fondly after her dog.

Maggie hid a grin. Winona had been a widow for many years. Maggie knew she spoiled the dog silly, treating him more like a child than a dog. Maggie suspected it was Winona who hated any change in her schedule; but she also felt that Winona's worry about the trauma caused to Samson was bothering her more than the discovery itself.

"Have you thought of a dog psychiatrist?" Maggie had always thought this profession rather a joke, but in this case it might be just the thing.

"Yes, I have." Winona turned eagerly to Maggie. "Do you know one?"

"Uh, no, I don't. But I've heard about them on TV. Have you asked your vet?"

"That's a good idea. I'll do that."

Winona had slowed her pace but now she began to move briskly once more, leaving Maggie lagging a little behind. Maggie had to hurry to catch up. Winona had a few years on her but she was obviously in excellent physical shape.

"Jonathan talked to Hal, you know. About buying that large parcel where we used to let the horses run." Maggie heard herself panting slightly from the effort of keeping up and scolded herself for neglecting her exercise. She'd have to get out more. Too much sitting around sewing.

But this news slowed Winona down once again. Her eyes widened. "Well, how do you like that. I wonder how Harley would have felt about that?"

Maggie was surprised at the question. "I know he and Ed never got along, but Jon was just a boy then."

Winona shook her head. "That's not what I meant." But Maggie's train of thought seemed to interest her more.

"Didn't you ever wonder *why* Harley and Ed didn't get along?"

Maggie shrugged. "Personality, I suppose. Ed was a strange one. I never got to know him well. And Harley's a bit eccentric, though he's usually polite."

"Something Ed wasn't, you mean."

Maggie didn't respond. She didn't know what Winona was getting at. They both knew that Ed Hunter had been a disagreeable man.

"Best thing ever happened to Carmen, him running off like that." Winona called to Samson, who was sniffing too close to a jumping cholla. He trotted obediently back to his mistress's side.

"I saw Carmen yesterday. She's been in town; she came to see Jon perform. She rented an apartment for the run of the play so she'll be around for a while yet." Maggie tripped over a loose rock and had to scramble to keep her footing. "From what she said, I think she would have loved to live with Jon and take care of him. What she said about Jon, however, leads me to think he preferred to live alone."

They walked along for a moment, the only sound the noise of their boots against the dry desert soil. Warmth was seeping into Maggie's shoulders as they walked along the trail, the rising sun at their backs.

Maggie decided to go back to Winona's earlier question about Ed and Harley. "So what's your opinion on why Ed and Harley didn't get on?"

Winona continued her steady stride, but Maggie noticed a small smile. "Like you said, Harley is a strange one, but he's nice and polite. Knows how to treat a woman, even if he's not much of a talker. But that Ed Hunter . . ." Winona's scowl was fierce. "That was one ornery cuss. Nasty temper."

Maggie couldn't say much to counter this. She agreed with every word.

"People didn't talk about that stuff then like they do now.

But don't you think Ed probably beat up on Carmen? Maybe even Jon."

Maggie frowned. "We used to talk some about it. And I think we all agreed that he might have."

Winona nodded, satisfied. "Now this is just speculation, but I always thought Harley was a little sweet on Carmen. Or maybe he just saw Ed hit her or something and got protective. Whatever it was, there was no love lost between Ed and Harley. But Harley always treated Carmen like a queen. And he never much cared for kids, but he treated Jon nicely. For him."

Maggie thought this over while she trailed after Winona. It made some sense, and was as much of a possibility as anything else. She did remember things in much the way Winona described. Still, Harley and Carmen as a couple was not something she'd ever considered. Yet Harley had been very interested in hearing about Carmen. And Carmen's eyes had lit up at mention of Harley.

She was so busy searching her memory for any incidences of the two of them together, she almost didn't hear Winona.

"When's the funeral?"

Maggie was surprised at the sudden question. Especially when she realized that in all the time they'd spent together, Carmen hadn't mentioned this. "I don't know. Carmen didn't say anything about the funeral, or even if they released the body to her." Maggie couldn't believe she hadn't thought to ask Carmen about this. "She asked me earlier to help with the arrangements, but she was pretty upset when I saw her yesterday. Do you want me to call you when I find out? I don't know if it will be here in town. They did live in L.A. a lot longer than they did here."

Winona said she would like to know, so Maggie promised to give her a call. She said a quick good-bye—Winona wasn't one to linger over greetings, whether hello or good-bye—then mounted Chestnut, checking her watch. She should be able to get to St. Rose at approximately her usual time.

She took one last glance back at Winona and Samson walking along the old trail. Maggie had been thinking recently that she should get herself a dog. They'd always had one when the boys were young, but she'd left the last dog at the house with Hal when she'd moved into her condo. A big, bouncy golden retriever, he would have been terribly out of place in the small condo.

Now, looking after Winona and Samson, Maggie decided she'd rethink it. Would she become a dotty old lady who doted on her dog, treating it like a baby instead of an animal? Heaven forbid!

Maggie was still watching the retreating forms when Winona stopped, stooping to pat Samson's head. The dog looked intently into her face as she talked to him. Then she straightened and they continued on their way.

Maggie looked after them for another minute before turning Chestnut and heading back toward the barn. But her mind was still on Winona and her poor traumatized cocker. She shook her head and urged Chestnut into a trot. If she ever got that silly over an animal, she hoped Hal would have her committed!

Chapter Eleven

Maggie arrived at the Quilting Bee a little later than usual. The others were situated around the frame, stitching while they listened to Anna describe the First Communion dress she was making for her granddaughter. But Maggie's appearance had them leaving that topic for the more interesting one of murder. They allowed Maggie to store her purse in the closet and seat herself at the frame. But she'd barely gotten her needle threaded when Clare spoke.

"Victoria said you went to the show again last night," she began. "But she wouldn't say much else."

"I told them I wanted to wait until you were here," Victoria explained. "Most of the information is yours to give, anyway."

Maggie began by telling them about Carmen's visit. "You should have seen Carmen when she arrived." Maggie tugged at the thread she was drawing through the quilt, then smoothed the fabric with her finger. "She's very tidy, her hair and makeup always just so. She's over fifty, but normally you'd never know it to look at her. But when she stepped into my house yesterday, she looked every bit of it. Her hair was messed and her dress rumpled. And of course her eyes were red and her makeup either gone or smeared. She was terribly upset."

"Oh, dear, that poor woman." Anna was beginning to tear up herself just thinking about the distraught mother.

"But why was she so upset?" Clare wanted to know.

"Well, the detective in charge of the case had stopped by to see her. When she called me the other day, she said they wanted to see her again, and she thought she would just go down to the police station one day. When she found out about claiming the body," she added.

"What an awful business that would be," Louise murmured.

"She wanted me to go with her, for moral support she said."

"Oh, I can understand that," Anna said with a shudder. "I could never do that alone."

"So the detective went to her house instead?" Clare wanted them to get back on the subject.

Maggie nodded. "She claimed he practically accused her of killing Jon. But I think she was just upset, and when they asked where she was at the time of the murder, she took it the wrong way. It seems to me they would want to ask that of everyone who knew him whether they are suspects or not."

"I'll bet not too many people have alibis for the time he was killed," Louise pointed out. "Most people would have been in bed asleep when it happened, and how can you prove that?"

"Did he have life insurance?" Edie asked. "If he did, his mother was probably the beneficiary since he wasn't married. And if a lot of money is involved . . ."

Anna gasped in shock, Maggie's eyes widened at the suggestion, and Victoria looked ill at the thought of a mother harming her child. Clare and Louise just stared.

"Now don't you look at me that way," Edie admonished. "You might not like the idea, but you know as well as I do that it happens all the time. Why, the newspapers are always full of stories about mothers hurting their children, and even killing them."

Louise nodded thoughtfully. "That is true, Edie, but oftentimes those women have serious psychological problems. And the last few cases I've read about have involved newborns. That is a little different from killing a son you've lived with and loved for the past thirty years."

Edie dismissed this with her usual "Humph." She knotted her thread and deftly sunk the knot into the batting. "I don't think most of those people are really sick. It's just a ploy on the part of their lawyers to try to get them off."

Louise, with her background as a nurse, was ready to deny this, but Maggie forestalled her with a comment of her own. "I just can't see Carmen doing anything like that. She lived for that boy. She told me she traveled around, making short visits to the cities where he was appearing so that she could see him act. She does private-duty nursing so she can control her schedule. She did it on her own, she said; sometimes he didn't even know she was there."

Louise looked up sharply at this last. "Didn't he want her there?"

Maggie looked troubled. "I don't know. Being with Carmen again made me realize how little I ever really knew her. I'm more confused than ever about her relationship with Jonathan. And also, his relationship with the other actors."

"Did she talk about the other actors?" Clare was all interest.

"Yes and no. She made some general comments that really didn't tell me anything. But she did mention he'd been dating Tanya—for quite some time. She called her a hussy, actually, and said Jon claimed she was flirting with all the other guys on the set. But I wasn't sure how to react to that after she told me she thought Jon didn't want her staying with him because of Tanya. He did invite Carmen to come and see him perform here, though," she added.

" 'Curiouser and curiouser,' " Victoria quoted.

Maggie nodded. "I don't think he was engaged to Tanya. Surely the other cast members would have known about something like that. And no one mentioned it. I do think Judy might have if they were that serious."

Louise agreed. "He was a young man, good-looking and with steady employment. He probably didn't want his mother living with him."

Edie smirked, then startled the others with her pronouncement. "You hadn't mentioned that Carmen was a nurse. That would make it easy for her to kill someone. She would know just where to hit a man to kill him."

Anna sucked in her breath with a noisy rasp.

Louise frowned, but it was apparent that she agreed.

Maggie didn't even want to think about it. A mother. Her old friend. Thankfully, Clare changed the subject. Still caught up with her idea involving the understudy, she didn't care to consider Carmen as the killer.

"I'm still wondering what happened to Jon's car," Clare said. "If the police found it, they've managed to keep it out of the papers. The carjacker theory is a pretty good one, except that the car should have turned up by now if it was true."

"They probably took it down to Mexico," Edie offered. She was good at looking at the downside of things, so her insight might presumably be good in this instance. "They'd never find it there, especially if it was sold for parts."

Maggie nodded. "Michael suggested as much on Monday night."

Edie looked smug at having her theory confirmed by an authority.

Louise was more practical. "It doesn't seem like they would break down a nice off-road vehicle like that. It would be a good car for driving in the desert either here or in Mexico. Seems to me they would try to sell it as is."

Victoria, a former teacher, offered a literary slant to the question. "Where do you hide something if you don't want it to be found?" she asked. "Remember Poe's 'Purloined Letter'?"

"That's right," Louise said. "You hide it in plain sight."

Victoria agreed. "It could be in a garage or a parking lot anywhere, right here in the valley. Though I suppose the police would have checked the obvious places like the airport." Her forehead wrinkled in thought. "And I guess the security people at the malls or parking garages would notice a car parked there day after day. But no one would think it strange to see a car in a garage, or even a carport. And if the garage had a door, well, no one would even see it. There are so many sport utility vehicles in the valley, who would notice a particular one?"

Maggie's hands stilled on the quilt, her mind working furiously. Her voice was soft and contemplative; she didn't even realize she was speaking out loud. "I wonder what kind of garage there is at Carmen's place? She drove a small Honda yesterday. It must be her own; it had California plates." She couldn't conceive of Carmen harming her own son, but Edie had planted that idea in her mind and now she was unable to exorcise it. Darn that Edie.

"Do you suppose the actors have cars here?" Clare asked. "They must be from all over the country."

"We're working again tonight," Victoria told them. "Maggie wants to get down there as much as possible and keep up the friendship with Judy."

"Oh, yes," Maggie remembered. "I told her about memory quilts and said we were interested in doing one for Carmen if the cast members would help out. She was going to ask them about getting together on Monday. That's the evening they don't perform," she reminded them.

Victoria smiled. "She promised them a barbecue at Hal's place."

"And we all get to come?" Clare asked, the excitement obvious in her voice. "Oh, how exciting!"

"I'm counting on all of you," Maggie informed them. "We'll have to sew all of the blocks and just have them ready for the actors to sign. Judy was quick to say that she didn't sew and she didn't know how many of the others could." Maggie snipped a thread and quickly cut another. "I told her if they were agreeable to a barbecue I'd issue a formal invitation that she could pass around or hang back-stage."

"You can do that tomorrow, when the family goes," Louise suggested.

"A barbecue with the actors from *Phantom of the Opera.*" Clare sighed. "I can hardly stand it," she declared, squeezing her shoulders together in a gesture of pure delight. "And I can meet the understudy myself." Clare was reluctant to give up her pet theory that the understudy had the most reason to want the star dead.

The others laughed, all except Edie. "I suppose we'll have to spend the weekend sewing up the blocks for them to sign."

Maggie wanted to glare at her, but forced herself to be polite. "You don't have to help if you're busy, Edie. The rest of us can handle it. We'll meet at my place on Saturday and work until it's done. I'll have lunch ready."

Edie muttered something about finding the time, and Louise hid a smile. "So what pattern will we use?" she asked.

For the rest of the morning, the women debated patterns and colors for the memory quilt. Clare was still excited about the upcoming barbecue when they began putting away the sewing things and covering the quilt.

"Remember, it's not set yet," Maggie warned. "I think we'll have it, but it will depend on Judy's reply."

"And Hal's." Victoria's gentle reminder brought the others up short.

"You mean you haven't asked him yet?" Anna asked. "Oh, my."

"Well, he's been out of town. He's due back today and I'll talk to him right away."

Clare wouldn't let the little details temper her elation at getting to meet real theater people. "Oh, wait till I tell Gerald. This is even better than television." A sudden thought brought a wide smile. "Why, it's just like 'Murder She

Wrote,' " she told Maggie. "And you're our Jessica Fletcher."

Everyone laughed. Even Edie.

"Heaven forbid," Maggie exclaimed. "No one will invite me over ever again." She laughed with the others at this reference to the television character's extraordinary ability to find dead bodies wherever she went.

"Better be careful," Louise added with a chuckle. "One of us might be next."

Victoria smiled with the others but her eyes were serious. "Yes, Maggie, you'd better be careful. Jessica Fletcher stumbled over most of those bodies herself."

Chapter Twelve

Hal greeted his mother with a kiss, accepting the applesauce bread she offered with thanks. Her grandsons ran in to see her, both of them shouting, each eager to recount wondrous tales of their Disney vacation. Goldie, their golden retriever, caught their excitement and writhed and wiggled among them, anxious to participate.

After a long visit with the family, a snack of her fresh bread—with milk for the children and coffee for the adults—and a shorter session of petting Goldie, Maggie was finally able to see Hal alone.

"So," she began, as they settled themselves in Hal's den. "Tell me about Jonathan Hunter's visit."

Hal smiled. He looked so much like his father when he grinned that way, it made Maggie teary. She wished Harry could have lived to see what fine men their sons had become.

"He called one day just before we left town. Said he heard I had some land for sale and would I show it to him. Just gave me his first name, so I figured he was wasting my time." Hal gestured to his mother, turning his hand in a manner that conveyed his mixed feelings at the time. "I mean just 'Jon.' But you never know, so I agreed to see him. I was surprised when he actually turned up the next day."

Hal shook his head, still incredulous. "That FOR SALE sign has produced some interesting results. Neighbors calling to ask what's happening. Every realtor and development company in the valley must have called. I've told them all I don't care to sell to a professional—I want to hold out for someone who will build a single-family home."

Maggie nodded.

"So you think Jon really was serious about buying the property."

Hal nodded. "I'd say so. He asked good, serious questions." He shook his head with a grin. "I didn't recognize him at all and when he finally told me his full name, and I realized he was our old playmate—well, I was pretty embarrassed."

Hal picked up his coffee cup and took a sip, grimacing when the now-cool liquid hit his tongue. He replaced the cup and smiled at his mother. "But he was great about it. Said it happens all the time. He can walk in and out of the theater without anyone knowing he's the star of the show. I thought that was interesting, since you always think of actors having so much ego. But he was cool about it."

"Did he say how he planned to pay for the land?"

Hal shook his head. "He didn't say, which made me wonder if he might be leading me on. Trying to look like a big man, you know—returning to his hometown as a big-time actor. I never really believed he would turn up with the financing or with cash for that matter, even though he assured me he would."

"And why didn't you let us know?"

Hal shrugged. "He asked me to keep it as our secret for now. Something about wanting to tell Michael himself. It sounded like a logical request to me, especially since it was by no means settled. I thought he might announce it when we saw him after the show on Friday."

Maggie nodded, but was unable to hide the emotion in her next statement. "I've been worried about you ever since I met Harley when I was out riding and he pointed out where the body was found. It's much too close for comfort."

Hal shrugged it off. "I don't think we have to worry here. I understand he was found on that road toward the rear of the property—that's not at all near the house."

"Still, it's too close for me to feel comfortable until it's solved."

Maggie cleared her throat. "I've been seeing some of the old neighbors. Carmen called me, you know."

"She did?" Hal was surprised. "Did you two keep in touch?"

"No. That's why I was so surprised. She asked me to go with her when she goes to claim the body." Maggie glanced down, somewhat embarrassed at what came next. "She said I was so strong, and that she needed to borrow some of that strength."

Hal agreed with Carmen's assessment. "You do have a strength of character that would appeal to a shy person. And from what I remember of Mrs. Hunter, she was very unprepossessing."

Maggie's eyes widened, yet she was proud that her son thought so well of her. You did the best you could and sometimes the results were wonderful. Hal had certainly become a prosperous yet caring young man, and her other sons had turned out just as well. And yet other women she knew had also done as best they could and their children caused them nothing but problems and heartache.

"So who else have you managed to run into?" The humor in his tone told her he knew she had engineered the meetings herself.

"Well, Winona Winthrop found the body, you know. Or, rather, Samson did." Maggie raised her brows in a way that showed her son just what she thought of dear Samson.

"Winona lives for that dog," Hal agreed. "Was she upset?"

"Only for dear Samson. Asked me if I knew of a dog psychologist."

Hal laughed and Maggie joined in. "And did you recommend one?"

Maggie chuckled. "I would have if I knew one." It felt good to laugh with Hal this way. She'd spent entirely too much time recently moping about and worrying.

While they enjoyed the thought of Samson reclining on

a psychologist's couch, Maggie took a few minutes to refresh their coffee. When she returned from the kitchen with the steaming cups, she again mentioned Winona. "She thinks Harley is fond of Carmen."

Hal thought this over while he enjoyed a sip of his hot coffee. Finally he shrugged. "I was too young when Carmen left to notice something like that. Harley is a grouchy old guy, but he can be thoughtful when he wants to be. Remember when the Appaloosa pony got caught in some barbed-wire fencing?"

Maggie nodded. The incident had happened a few years ago when the horse had gotten out of the corral. Some fencing had fallen during a storm and the horse had managed to tangle his ankles in the painful stuff.

"Well, Harley heard about the accident, and came over with some special ointment he'd mixed up. It worked great too." Hal leaned back in his chair, rubbing at the back of his neck. "Now that I'm back I expect he'll be calling again. He'll have heard that Jonathan was supposed to be buying that land, so he'll figure it's available."

"Again? You mean he's approached you before?"

"Oh, yeah." Hal was already explaining about Harley. "Came over as soon as the sign went up. Several of the neighbors called about this land. I would like to let him have it. Problem is, he doesn't have the money. Wants me to hang on to it until he can get it together, but he had no idea how long that might be. Knowing Harley, it might be forever."

Maggie nodded. Though, of course, you never knew. Look at that cleaning woman down South somewhere—it was just in the paper that she'd been saving for years and had donated a half million dollars to a local university for scholarship programs. For all her life she'd lived simply and worked at her cleaning. It was possible Harley had resources they knew nothing about. Maybe he, like the Southern cleaning woman, was sitting on a fortune. Though knowing Harley, Maggie thought, if there was a fortune, it was buried out in the desert somewhere behind his house.

"But why would he want it?" Maggie was thinking out loud rather than really asking Hal.

Hal shrugged. "I think he just wants it to have. Some people are funny about land."

Maggie nodded. "That could be. He's from the South, you know. And those Southerners are really attached to their land."

"I always thought Harley was a native; it's hard to imagine him anywhere else. When we were kids we used to call him 'the old prospector.' "

Maggie smiled at the name. "It fits him, but he is originally from the South."

"Well, I'd sell it to him tomorrow if he had the financing, but I can't afford to give this land away."

Maggie nodded. She understood. If they hadn't wanted the money the land would bring, they would have kept it in the family. She reached out and patted Hal on the arm. "It's okay. I know you would keep it if you could. But it will be all right."

Hal released a heavy sigh. "We could have the money quickly if I accepted one of the developers. But I really don't want to have that lot turned into a whole development. Some of these companies wouldn't think twice of putting four houses on an acre. And they always seem to have enough votes to change the zoning."

Maggie nodded sympathetically. She agreed wholeheartedly with Hal's sentiments. She stood up, still shaking her head over the complications Hal was facing. She collected the coffee cups and headed for the kitchen where Sara was busy preparing for dinner.

"Oh, dear." Maggie looked back, glad to see that Hal had followed her from the other room. "I almost forgot. I wanted to ask you about having a barbecue here on Monday evening." Quickly she told them about the memory quilt she wanted to make, and her idea of inviting all the actors over on Monday to sign it.

"Of course you can have the party here," Sara told her. "Hal will do his famous barbecue sauce, won't you, dear?"

Hal agreed that he would be happy to help out. "And I'm sure Sara and the boys will enjoy getting to meet all the actors as well."

"Actors? We get to meet actors?" The two boys had just come in from outside, catching their father's last line.

Maggie explained again.

"Wow. Cool," seven-year-old Joshua commented.

"Way cool," his ten-year-old brother agreed. "The Phantom. Wait till the guys hear."

The two boys raced from the room, each anxious to reach the telephone first to tell their friends the news.

Chapter Thirteen

Thursday evening found Maggie and Victoria once again making the short drive to Tempe. Victoria admitted to feeling tired this evening after so many late nights.

Maggie felt guilty. "Oh, dear. It's all my fault, dragging you down here with me every night."

"Don't be silly," Victoria reassured her. "I come of my own free will. You know how much I like this show. And I want to help find out who killed Jonathan if I can."

"You're a good friend, Victoria. I just hope that something comes of all these late nights. But I can't help thinking that getting to know Jon's associates will somehow help us arrive at the truth."

There was little more to say as they entered the theater parking lot.

The routine was familiar—the program stuffing, the greeting of patrons. Maggie noticed that Judy was still filling in for Tanya and that Susanne was also out.

Once the lights went out, Maggie became lost in the music. She was so deep in thought as she watched the actors on the stage that a late-arriving couple coming through her door startled her. Using her flashlight, she checked their tickets and directed them to the proper seats. Soon she'd be able to sit down herself. Volunteers could sit a half hour into the show, as long as there were empty seats along the aisle. Maggie had her eye on three empty seats at the end of the second row. She'd have a good view of the stage—and the actors—from there.

At the end of the first act, while she smiled at milling patrons and gave directions to the restrooms, Maggie decided that she would not be able to come to any great deductions about their personalities from observing the actors on stage. They were too good. They became the characters in long-ago Paris and she was unable to get any insight into their real character. And it did make her wonder. As Judy had said about Jon—he was a good actor. His image was part of the act. If any of these people were the murderer, how would she ever know? She would see whatever they wanted her to see. Perhaps Edie was right after all. They lied for a living.

By the time Maggie and Victoria met outside the stage door, Maggie was feeling thoroughly depressed. She'd decided halfway through the second act that it was arrogant of her to try to solve this crime. Just what did she think she was doing? She greeted Victoria without a smile. "Maybe we should just go on home."

Victoria's eyes widened in surprise. "What? Get into that traffic mess?" She turned to look out over the parking lot, which was swarming with the three thousand people who had lately been inside. Cars filled the traffic lanes, inching their way toward the exits. "Besides," she said, "I thought you were going to speak to Judy about the barbecue?"

The gentle reminder brought Maggie back to the moment. She had almost forgotten about her plans for the barbecue and the memory quilt. To lose sight of that, she must be even more tired than she cared to admit. And she genuinely liked the actors she had met so far. She wanted to go on with the party plans.

She smiled at Victoria. "Clare will kill me if I cancel the barbecue, so I'd better get on with it." Maggie took a step toward the stage door. Thinking of the memory quilt and of all the people who would work on it put a spring back into her step.

In this newfound spirit of optimism, Maggie smiled at the dancer who had just walked out. Lydia Osaki played

Meg, the opera dancer who was the main character's friend.

"Hello." Maggie thrust her hand out, and Lydia, after a momentary hesitation, shook it. "This is such a marvelous show. You do a very good job."

"Thank you. Didn't I see you talking to Judy the other night?"

"Yes. I knew Jonathan Hunter when he was a child, and I wanted to meet some of the people he'd been working with."

Lydia didn't say anything at this revelation, but continued to look at Maggie politely. Maggie wondered if Lydia's smile had lost some of its sparkle when she mentioned Jonathan, but thought it might just be her overactive imagination. "I was asking Judy about whether you all would be interested in helping to make a memory quilt for Jon's mother."

Lydia's smile returned. "Oh, yes. She did say something about that. And a western barbecue."

"That's right. I'm glad she mentioned it. I'm waiting for her now to hear what the reaction was." As Maggie finished speaking, Judy and Roman walked out. Judy greeted them without surprise.

"Hello. I thought I saw you right down front."

Maggie returned the friendly greeting. "Yes. I had a very nice seat. I never get tired of watching this show. The music is so wonderful. And your voice is fabulous."

"Is she for real?" Roman asked.

Judy laughed. "I'm going to make her president of my fan club."

Victoria smiled at the young woman. "Oh? Do you have a fan club here?"

Judy laughed again, Lydia and Roman joining in. "Wouldn't that be something," Roman commented.

"I don't have a fan club at all. But Maggie here is such an enthusiastic fan, I wouldn't mind if she started one." Judy bestowed a big grin on Maggie.

Maggie had to return the smile. She'd never had a daughter, but Judy was just the kind of person she would have wanted for one. Talk of a fan club, however, caught her interest. "Do you know if any of the others have fan clubs?"

Judy shook her head. "I was just kidding about a fan club. Fan clubs are pretty much a movie and TV thing. A touring company like this doesn't have a real star, because they're touring the play, not the individual actors."

Lydia agreed. "The company as a whole is good; we don't rely on one star to draw the audience."

Roman just nodded. He was very attractive, very muscular, and there was something extraordinarily graceful about the way he moved. But then he was a dancer; what she saw might just be a dancer's beauty of movement.

Maggie drew her eyes back to Judy. "From what I've been hearing about Jon, he seems the type who would have enjoyed a fan club."

Judy laughed. "Boy, you've got that right. He would have loved it. A bunch of teeny bopper girls who adored him—I guess you've got his number." Judy sobered, apparently just realizing that her statement contradicted the picture they had up to now tried to convey. "I guess you've figured out that he wasn't the little Boy Scout the papers tried to make him into after he died. He wasn't a bad guy, but he wasn't an angel, either." Judy exchanged looks with Lydia and Roman. "We were wondering if all this goody-goody stuff running in the paper would keep the police from finding his killer."

As a young woman with a program in her hand approached Roman, Maggie took Judy by the arm and moved toward the shrubbery, into the shadows and away from the people still clustered around the stage door. She lowered her voice as well. "Judy. Tell me the truth. Do you think someone in the company might have killed Jon?"

Maggie was glad to see that Judy didn't seem to resent the question. She considered for a moment before answering. "I don't like to think that one of us did it." She pursed her lips together and her fingers clenched tightly at the backpack that was flung over her shoulder. "But, in a fit of passion? Yeah, I think someone *could* have."

"A fit of passion?" Maggie repeated.

Judy nodded. "You know—during a fight or something. It happens. Actors are passionate people. Emotional. We're always flaring up at people. But it passes. Pretty quick normally." She tugged at the straps of the backpack once more, resettling it on her shoulder.

Maggie thought Judy looked unsettled, and wondered if it was because of her questions. She was being a nosy busybody, of course, and she knew it. But how else would she ever get anywhere? "I guess it's pretty impertinent of me to ask you about this." Impulsively, Maggie threw her arm around Judy and gave her a hug. "You're a special person to let me do this, and actually answer truthfully instead of telling me to mind my own business."

To her surprise, Judy hugged her back. "I hope you won't take this the wrong way, but you remind me of my grandmother. It's your personality, I think, though I first thought of it when you mentioned quilts."

"Oh, dear, that's right." Maggie shook her head. "I can't seem to remember anything these days. I was waiting for you to ask about the memory quilt and the barbecue."

"What's this about a barbecue?"

While they were talking, Jeff had come outside, signed a few autographs, and was now standing beside them. Lydia and Roman were still there, too, with Lydia and Victoria deep in conversation.

"Did Judy ask all of you about coming to a barbecue at my ranch on Monday? I've spoken to my son and his wife, and they're looking forward to it."

"Oh, yes, she did. It sounds good," Jeff assured her. "Home-cooked food." An expression of pure bliss appeared on his handsome face, quickly changing to deep sadness.

"And of course we all want to help you do the quilt for Mrs. Hunter."

"Though she was pretty much a thorn in the side as far as Jon was concerned," Lydia commented.

Maggie turned toward Lydia. "She was?"

While the other actors stabbed her with their sharp looks, Lydia just shrugged and continued speaking to Maggie. "Oh, yeah. He was always complaining about how she hovered around all the time. She followed the show from city to city, you know."

Maggie nodded. She'd heard as much from Carmen. "She thinks he didn't know."

Lydia gave a short laugh. "Oh, he knew. But he pretended he didn't because that way he didn't have to see her or entertain her while she was in the city. And he definitely didn't want to have to invite her to stay with him."

"Carmen said as much. She thought he was with Tanya all the time."

The others were so obviously surprised at this, that Maggie had her confirmation of its untruth.

"We thought it was probably just a case of a young man wanting to be on his own," Victoria said.

Lydia suddenly looked embarrassed. "I guess I've said enough. I'd better go."

She glanced around the area near the stage door. "Where did Roman go? He was just here."

"He probably left with one of the others," Jeff suggested.

The others were nodding agreement when Duane, the house manager, opened the stage door and looked out. He seemed surprised to see them all standing there, but disappeared back inside without comment.

Judy checked her watch. "Look at the time. Shouldn't you ladies be in bed?"

"Yes, we really should," Victoria agreed. "Come on, Maggie. Let's get going and let these nice people get home, too."

"Stop again next time you work the show," Judy told them. She and the others waved and headed down the path.

Walking across the driveway toward their car, Maggie told Victoria about her brief private conversation with Judy. There were still a few people moving around in the large parking lot and lights kept the shadows from being too dark. "Even though I didn't learn anything earth-shattering, it's interesting that Judy believes one of the company could have done it."

Victoria agreed. "Speaking of passion, I thought it was interesting, the expression on Jeff's face when he came out and saw you talking to Judy. It was such a quick thing, I could almost have imagined it, but I swear there was a second there when he was highly irritated at seeing you."

They reached the car just as Victoria finished speaking, and Maggie was thoughtful as she climbed into the driver's seat. "I'm afraid Edie's right," Maggie admitted. "They are all such good actors there's no way of knowing whether or not they're telling the truth."

She was inserting her key, ready to start the car, when she saw a slip of paper under the windshield wiper in front of her. With a sigh she climbed back out to retrieve it, grumbling all the while.

"Why do people do this? Don't they realize how irritating it is to find ads stuck in your window when you're ready to drive off?"

But as she settled back into her seat, it was obvious that the paper wasn't the ad she expected. It was a plain sheet of white paper, torn at one end and folded in half—an obvious note. On it, in felt-tip marker and block letters, was a cryptic message: *"Butt out, lady—or else!"*

Chapter Fourteen

Maggie felt the blood drain out of her face as her heart seemed to stop its steady beat then restart at twice its usual rate. She stared at the scrap of paper, scarcely able to believe that someone would threaten her.

"Oh, dear."

Victoria's understated comment was enough to throw Maggie over the edge. But she caught the gasp before it escaped with a hand to her mouth. The hand holding the note trembled, despite her best efforts to steady it.

"We have to call the police," Victoria told her, putting her hand on the door handle.

But Maggie stopped her. "No. Close the door." Maggie made sure all the doors were locked. "I want to leave. We'll call Michael." Not giving Victoria any more of a chance to object, she started the engine and pulled out of the parking space.

Victoria quickly refastened her seat belt. "He won't like it," she warned.

Victoria's quiet warning turned out to be a gross understatement. Michael was furious. Of course, fear for his mother was a major contributing factor.

"You should have reported this right away, right there in the parking lot before you moved the car." Michael had slipped the note into a plastic storage bag and he held it in his hand as he paced before his mother and her friend. "You read all those mystery novels—don't you know anything about crime scenes? And not disturbing them?"

He stopped his pacing to stand before his mother with a worried, accusatory look in his eyes. His fisted hands lay on his hips, the clear plastic bag still gripped in his fingers. "Just what have you been doing that would get you a warning like this?"

"I don't know." Maggie's voice oozed sincerity. That part was easy; she honestly didn't know. "Victoria and I just did our job ushering. Then we waited at the stage door to say hello to Judy."

Michael's eyes narrowed. "Judy?"

Maggie nodded. "Judy Noonan. She's the actress who is playing Carlotta until Tanya Kessler gets back."

Now that Michael was here, taking charge of things, she felt better. The drive home had been awful, with a spring storm arising out of nowhere with fierce winds that drove huge raindrops into the windshield. The storm had appeared as suddenly as the horrible slip of paper and disappeared before they arrived at her home. If only the slip of paper could have disappeared as well.

Michael was still staring at her. Finally, he shook his head, quick and hard, like a dog shedding water. "When you left the stage door . . . were there still people in the lot when you got to the car?"

Both women nodded. "Oh, yes. Victoria even commented on it, didn't you?"

"Do you know if many people were still left backstage?"

Maggie shook her head slowly back and forth, thinking. "I think Judy may have been one of the last ones out. We moved away from the door itself to talk, so I really don't know for sure. But we did see Duane peek out, and we thought at that time that everyone was gone."

"Actually, Jeff came out last," Victoria said. "Remember? You were talking to Judy, off at the side of the path. I was still with Lydia and Roman. Jeff came out, signed some autographs, then went over to you and Judy. That's when you mentioned the barbecue and we all came together again."

"You're right." Maggie turned to Michael. "I'm having a barbecue at Hal's Monday evening. For the cast members. We're making a memory quilt for Carmen, and they're all going to sign blocks. You're invited."

Maggie was beginning to feel better. Almost normal. Coming home had definitely been the right thing to do. Victoria made tea while she called Michael, and the hot drink had soothed her so that she could talk to him now without fear of breaking down. She was even beginning to feel hungry.

"How about some gingerbread?" she asked, getting up to fetch the white rabbit cookie jar from the counter. "Megan and I made gingerbread cookies over the weekend." Maggie couldn't believe that it had been only five days since she and her granddaughter had laughed together in this same kitchen, rolling out gingerbread cookie dough.

Michael watched her set out dessert plates and shook his head. "I can't believe you're hungry."

"I'm surprised myself, but it has been a long time since dinner." Maggie bit into a gingerbread bear, glad she hadn't sent all the cookies home with Megan. Gingerbread did taste very good with a hot cup of tea.

Michael stood beside the two women, refusing to sit at the table with them. He said he liked to pace, that it helped him think, but Maggie suspected he liked the height advantage. So he could loom over them while he scolded her and dictated what she ought to do and not do.

"You stay out of this case, Mother. Let the police do their jobs." He ran his hand through his hair, then leaned down over the table near Maggie. "Maybe you'd better stop visiting those actors after the show."

Maggie wanted to object, but he frowned at her and she decided to refrain.

"Get to bed now, and try to sleep, then go on to the church in the morning the way you always do. Then come back here and bake more cookies or something. I'll stop by after my shift. Okay?"

Maggie nodded. When he was in this mood, he was just like his father. He wouldn't budge a bit, no matter what she said. So she'd nod, then go about her regular business. But she would be home when he stopped by.

"Remember tomorrow—or today, rather," she said, glancing at the clock, "is Friday. We're all going to the theater tonight."

Michael cut off an expletive, but Maggie went on.

"I promised to take the boys to the stage door to meet some of the actors."

Michael turned a frustrated look toward his mother but didn't say anything. Seeing his blue eyes turn a stormy gray, Maggie thought he was purposely refraining from comment. "Don't worry," she told him. "We'll all be there together. Nothing will happen."

Maggie prayed her brave words would hold true while Michael hugged her good-bye. He then left with Victoria, volunteering to walk her home since it was so late. Maggie watched them exit, locked the door behind them and shuffled back into the kitchen. She no longer had to put on a brave face. But she did try to keep her mind off the note as she busied herself tidying an already tidy kitchen.

Finally, she moved toward the bedroom. It was after 1:00, the night beyond her windows dark and silent. The fearsome wind that had so bothered her on the drive home had passed. She was alone, and for the first time in many years, Maggie wished dearly for another live body in her home. Maybe she would have to look into getting a dog after all. She was sure she could have one without spoiling it like Winona did hers. After all, Victoria had a cat, and she didn't treat it like a baby.

Even though Maggie took her time getting ready, she was settling into her bed in what seemed like a very short time. Tonight, she didn't lie in bed waiting for elusive sleep to overtake her. She reached immediately into the nightstand and closed her fingers over the cool beads of her rosary. Memories of Harry and his gift overwhelmed her, as did the shock of finding that note tucked under her windshield wiper blade. But she forced away the tears that threatened and wrapped the turquoise beads through her fingers. With determination and faith, she began to repeat her prayers.

Chapter Fifteen

The Quilting Bee was working under the olive tree in the courtyard when Maggie and Victoria made their belated appearance on Friday morning. It was a beautiful desert spring morning. The sun shone in a clear blue sky and the temperature was still in the seventies. The shade of the old olive tree protected the women and their quilt from the sun's ultraviolet rays, and they were cool and comfortable.

It was Victoria's turn to drive this morning, but due to the excitement of the previous evening and the lateness of the hour when she finally got to bed, she'd overslept. Maggie had awakened her with a call just forty minutes ago and she was still feeling flustered.

"Sorry we're late. I overslept, I'm afraid."

"It doesn't matter," Louise assured her. "It's not as if we're punching a time clock here."

Maggie and Victoria settled into the chairs that were sitting empty at the frame.

"You must have needed the extra sleep," Anna assured Victoria. "But, Maggie dear, you really look exhausted. Are you getting enough sleep?"

Maggie sighed. "No, I haven't been."

"It's all this worry about crime," Edie declared. "I'm surprised any of us can get any sleep these days. And when murder happens so close to Maggie's son's home. . . ." Edie's voice trailed off, leaving them to imagine what awful things they would.

"Oh, dear." Clare's brows drew together as she glanced worriedly across at Maggie. "It's our fault, isn't it? We've all got you chasing around trying to find out who killed Jonathan Hunter."

"It's not your fault," Maggie reassured her. "I'm just trying to resolve things in my mind. I'd probably be doing it anyway. But last night was different." She sighed again as she punched her needle into the quilt top, then purposely slowed to take the series of little stitches that created the quilting. Maggie found quilting very relaxing, but sometimes she had to put a little effort into purging disrupting thoughts.

With a few words as possible, Maggie proceeded to tell the others about her evening at the theater. When she finally got to the note on the windshield of her car, there were several gasps and more commiserating comments.

"Oh, dear," Anna said. "You should stop right away, before something happens."

"Told you," Edie intoned in her dry voice. "Not safe anywhere these days."

Victoria had just finished recounting what Michael said about the incident, when Carmen appeared at the courtyard gate. Since Maggie sat facing the entrance, she saw her immediately and got up to welcome her. At least outwardly. Inwardly, she was so tired, she wished Carmen had stayed at home. She wasn't sure she could handle any more surprises, and so far, Carmen had been just full of them.

Maggie greeted Carmen warmly, then led her over to the quilt frame where she introduced her to the others. After the hellos and the expressions of sympathy, they all settled back down to their work. Anna went to the quilt room and returned shortly with a wooden hoop filled with a sample quilt sandwich. It was what they used to help teach a new member who wanted to join the Quilting Bee.

Anna sat with Carmen at one side of the frame, demonstrating the proper way to take a quilting stitch, while Maggie turned the conversation to the memory quilt party.

"I spoke to Judy last night and the barbecue is all set. So now I have to decide on a pattern for the memory quilt, then maybe some of you could come over to my place tomorrow and help me cut the blocks."

"Do you mean Judy Noonan?" Carmen asked, looking up from her work.

"Yes," Maggie replied. "She's been very friendly, and I feel I've gotten to know her over the past few days."

Carmen didn't comment, instead turning her attention to the sewing in her lap. Anna had watched her first few stitches, declared them excellent, and said Carmen just needed some practice.

"I can tell you have some experience sewing," Anna told her before slipping back into place at the frame and picking up her abandoned needle.

"Maggie is going to have a barbecue for the cast members at her son's ranch," Clare explained to Carmen. "So that everyone can sign the blocks for the memory quilt."

"I think black would be good as a main color in the quilt," Louise suggested. "It really does bring to mind the Phantom, don't you think?"

"After we talked about it yesterday, I checked my fabric stash and I have some wonderful black prints," Clare said.

Victoria agreed. "Black and white would be nice. Maybe some red accents."

Maggie turned to Carmen. "Black and white does sound attractive to me. I've seen some lovely black-and-white quilts. What do you think, Carmen?"

Carmen looked up. "I'm afraid I don't know much about this kind of thing, Maggie. I'm sure whatever you decided will be beautiful. That quilt you're working on is lovely."

They all stopped a moment to gaze at the fan quilt. The quilting was progressing at a good pace, and it was looking better every day. All the fans were pieced with blue prints, the background a creamy white-on-white. Into the plain white blocks between the pieced fans, they were quilting a fan decorated with roses. The border had already been rolled over, and just a large rectangle at the center was left undone.

With various expressions of pride and contentment, the Bee members returned to their work. Carmen, too, bent her head to her practice stitching. But she quickly surprised them with a comment, made quietly and seemingly directed down into her quilt hoop.

"I talked to Father Bob about having Jon's funeral mass here tomorrow."

"Here?"

"Tomorrow?"

Carmen looked around at the varying expressions of surprise and sympathy. "Jon always talked about Scottsdale and how happy he was here. And then he had planned to buy some land and build a house. At least that's what Maggie and the police told me." She balanced the hoop in her lap, reaching into a pocket for a folded tissue which she used to dab at her eyes. "He hadn't told me about it, but he probably wanted to surprise me."

Maggie and Louise exchanged looks. Maggie had wondered previously if Carmen was deluding herself about her son. Was he planning to invite her to live with him? What kind of relationship did Carmen and Jon have?

"So he'll be buried here in town?" Maggie asked.

Carmen nodded. "Yes. I've been making the arrangements. I know I'd asked you to help, Maggie, but it turned out I was grateful for the distraction. It's kept me busy these past few days."

Anna's eyes filled with tears as she watched Carmen. "You're being very brave," she assured her.

"It will be a small funeral," Carmen continued. "I don't think I'll have viewing hours or a rosary. We don't know enough people here who would come. The cast members will be tied up with the show tonight, and then all day tomorrow. So I asked Father Bob about just having the mass tomorrow morning, then a blessing at the grave."

"Well, I'll come, of course," Maggie said. "And I'm sure Michael will want to. Did you call him?"

"No. I thought you would tell him. I didn't have his number," Carmen explained. She was staring down at the fabric in the quilt hoop, studying the stitches on the fabric as though it was a valuable museum piece.

Maggie was beginning to wonder about Carmen. Could she really be as incompetent as she appeared? It wouldn't have been difficult to contact Michael, and as her son's only local friend, it would certainly have been the proper thing to do.

"We'll all come," Clare said. She looked at the others to see if they agreed and there were nods all around. "Then we can all head over to Maggie's to work on the memory quilt afterward," she added.

"Oh, dear. I guess I should have something afterward . . ." Carmen suddenly seemed to realize this was the common practice.

The women reassured Carmen that she needn't have a reception after the funeral. "Everyone knows you're from out-of-town. No one will expect to go to your place afterward," Maggie told her.

"You are all so nice," Carmen said. "At a time like this I miss not having close friends. I had Maggie when we lived here, of course, but I never seemed to make good friends after we moved. I guess I was embarrassed about Ed leaving that way. I didn't know what to say when people asked about my husband. And in recent years I've done a lot of traveling, so it's been even harder."

Maggie saw Victoria send a questioning glance her way at hearing Carmen claim her as a best friend. Maggie raised her eyebrows and shrugged. She'd never felt she was particularly close to Carmen. But obviously, Carmen had no one else.

"I'll have to check over my patterns for autograph blocks," Maggie said, changing the subject.

"We were just talking about this." Clare turned to Carmen to explain about her own autograph quilt. "I'm making a quilt for my family reunion. We had exchanged some patterns for classic autograph blocks and I picked one of the most popular." She turned back to Maggie. "Have you decided which block you'll use?"

Maggie shook her head. "I've been so busy, I haven't decided. But actually, since we don't have a lot of time, I think a plainer block would be a good idea. There's one in one of my quilt books—like a rail fence block. It's just three strips of fabric, white in the center and then a print on either side. The quilt is very attractive, but it's done in multicolored scraps."

"Do you think it would be as nice in just black and white?" Anna asked.

"We could add grays as well," Victoria suggested. "I have some lovely gray prints."

Everyone nodded. They would all bring their black and gray prints with them the next day to have a good variety of fabric.

"Will you be returning to L.A. soon?" Louise asked Carmen.

Maggie was wondering the same thing. Once the funeral was over, would there be any reason for Carmen to stay?

"I haven't decided yet." Carmen pressed her needle into the cloth and lay the hoop on her lap. "This is such a nice group you ladies have here. I wonder if there's something similar in L.A. I should look into it."

Maggie heard a wistful note in Carmen's voice that pulled at her heart.

Carmen must have heard it, too. She straightened her spine, and her voice became more assured. "There must be some church group there that I can join. I'm afraid I haven't been too active in my church these past years."

"There are quilt groups all over the country," Anna assured her. "And quilters are such nice people. I've always looked for a quilt group to join whenever I moved to a new place."

"You have your job there, don't you?" Louise asked.

"I am registered with an agency there, yes," Carmen replied. "I do private-duty nursing, you see, so my jobs and hours vary. Sometimes I live in. Quite often, actually."

"Wow. Do you work for famous people there?" Clare wanted to know.

Carmen smiled. "Sometimes. I can't talk about clients, of course. It wouldn't be right."

"Oh, of course not," Clare hastened to agree. Still, Maggie could see that Carmen had gone up in her estimation. Clare was probably imagining her nursing some elderly movie star.

Carmen gathered up her sewing things and stood, placing everything carefully on her chair. Maggie rose, too, wondering if Carmen was ready to leave.

"I have to get over to the funeral home. I'm sure you understand," she said, her eyes moving around the the frame. "It was nice meeting all of you ladies and I thank you for showing me how to quilt. I'd like to try it again sometime."

As the others murmured their good-byes, Maggie moved forward to walk Carmen to her car.

"You've been so wonderful, Maggie," Carmen told her as they walked across the courtyard toward the gate. "I just don't know what I'd have done without you."

"Well, you seem to have done just fine setting up the funeral and everything," Maggie reminded her. "You did all that yourself."

Carmen dismissed this with a wave of her hand. "Oh, most of that was suggested by the mortician. And Father Bob was a big help." Carmen sighed. "I'm afraid I'm not much of an organizer on my own. I just don't know how I'll manage without Jon."

"But he hasn't lived at home for a long time now, has he?"

"No, but he kept in touch." Carmen's voice had taken on a harder edge, becoming more insistent. Who was she trying to convince? Maggie wondered.

"Well, I'm sure you'll manage just fine," Maggie told her. "We women are very resilient creatures. I was sure I'd go to pieces when my Harry died, but I managed just fine."

Carmen patted her arm. "Of course you did. I wouldn't have expected anything less. But then you're so different from me, Maggie."

"I don't think so. After all, you managed very well after Ed left. You had a child to support, and you worked and finished your education. And you both turned out well." Maggie smiled at Carmen and squeezed her hand, still resting on her arm. "You just have to tell yourself you can manage, and you will," Maggie insisted.

"I'll try," Carmen told her. They had reached the parking lot and Carmen unlocked the door of her car.

Maggie put her arm around Carmen's shoulders. "You take care now. I'll see you tomorrow."

"Thank you." Carmen looked ready to cry and she hastened into the car.

Maggie watched her drive off. She just couldn't quite figure her out. Was she as shy and unable to manage as she tried to have them believe? But, as Maggie had pointed out to her, Carmen had survived her husband's desertion—by moving hundreds of miles away and then raising a young child on her own and continuing with her schooling as well.

Maggie shook her head as she headed back inside. Maybe Jon got some of his acting skills from his mother. Lately, when Maggie was around Carmen she had a feeling she was watching a performance. The poor, distressed mother. The helpless female. The deserted wife. Now if only Maggie could figure out which one was the real Carmen.

Chapter Sixteen

Maggie sat in the dark theater between her two grandsons, letting the beautiful music wash over her. She never tired of hearing this score. The boys were mesmerized by the Phantom character, currently stalking the heroine as he sang. They had been suitably startled when the chandelier exploded at the beginning of the show and Maggie looked forward to seeing their reactions to it dropping. Megan, uncertain how she felt about the masked man on stage, sat a few seats away, her head snuggled into her mother's shoulder.

Maggie let herself feel the wonderful music and spent more time watching her relations than watching the show. She enjoyed seeing the children's reactions to the special effects and couldn't help sneaking peeks at her sons now and again. She couldn't ever remember taking them to a Broadway show, but then as boys they had been more interested in rodeos than in musicals.

After the show, Maggie led the way to the stage door. She'd told the boys about meeting some of the actors and how they all knew Uncle Michael's friend who had been the Phantom. She'd bought the handsome souvenir programs for each of her three grandchildren and fished through her purse for pens so that they could collect autographs.

Jason and Joshua were immediately impressed by the friendly smiles thrown Maggie's way by the departing musicians and actors. Megan and Jason were busy getting the autographs of two ballerinas when Judy appeared, greeting Maggie with warmth.

"You know my grandma?" young Joshua asked, the awe in his voice evident. He had already gotten the ballerinas to sign his book, and now held his pen out to Judy. "Do you know the Phantom, too, Grandma?"

Judy laughed, a rich throaty sound that had Michael turning toward her. "Yes, I do know your grandma. And the Phantom knows her, too." She had just begun to scribble her name on the program when she stopped. "Jeff," she called.

The tall man who had just stepped from the stage door maneuvered around some young people and moved toward her. Maggie was sure she saw him frown, but by the time he reached them, he had a pleasant smile on his face. Judy latched onto his arm, turning him toward Joshua, who had now been joined by his brother and his cousin.

"Here he is, guys. The Phantom himself." She smiled at Jeff. "Tell these guys that you know Maggie here."

Jeff's smile widened. "Sure. Maggie and I are old friends." He put his arm around Maggie's shoulder and gave her a friendly squeeze. "And who are you?" He smiled at Joshua as he took the program and pen he held forward.

"Wow. I'm Joshua. This is my grandma." His eyes were huge as he stared at the man who had played the part he'd so admired. But he stepped closer to Maggie. He was pleased to meet the Phantom but unsure of the character and his relationship to this man. "You were kind of scary."

Jeff laughed. "I hope so. And do you like scary?" He handed back his program and took the one proffered by Joshua's brother.

Joshua nodded. Then, feeling more important than he had in all his seven years, he introduced the Phantom to his brother Jason.

Behind the children, Maggie spoke to Judy. "I've arranged with Hal and Sara to have the barbecue at six on

Monday evening. Will that be all right? I thought you might enjoy an early night for a change."

Judy nodded. "That sounds fine. I've been spreading the word and everyone is looking forward to it."

Maggie searched in her purse, finally retrieving a large white envelope. "Here's the invitation I made up. Maybe you can post it somewhere backstage where everyone will see it." She searched the faces of the people crowded around the stage door. "Come and meet Hal and his wife." She pushed through the young people collecting autographs, and stopped near her sons. All four of them stood together, watching the children and their mother with bemused expressions. Their wives stood beside them.

"Judy Noonan, I want you to meet my sons. . . ." She introduced Judy to all her boys and their wives, Hal and Frank pointing out their children.

"What a beautiful family you have, Maggie." Judy winked at her, leaning in closer. "Such handsome sons, too."

Maggie laughed, proud of her sons and their families and liking Judy more each time she saw her. "They're pretty good guys—most of the time."

As the men and especially their wives laughed, Michael approached Judy and said something Maggie didn't hear. She started to move closer but stopped when Sara asked about the upcoming barbecue. Maggie relayed the information she'd gotten earlier from Judy. By the time she'd finished and looked back around, Michael and Judy had disappeared.

Frank held Megan on his shoulder, half asleep now that the excitement was over, and he was shooing his two nephews toward the cars. The hour was late, he told the kids, and the actors were surely tired after their performance. And they had two performances the next day. Reluctantly, the children followed their parents to the parking lot.

Bobby escorted Merrie across the driveway, Sara walking with them. Hal was waiting for her, Maggie realized. She took one last glance back.

Jeff was standing with a young couple. The woman's adoring eyes were on him, her escort watching with resigned acceptance. Jeff, Maggie could tell, was enjoying himself. What young man wouldn't?

Maggie remembered Clare's oft-repeated theory about the understudy having the most reason to kill the star of the show. Jeff seemed to be a nice young man. But he was also an excellent actor. And she kept catching glimpses of a more emotional side—of what might be an anger kept under tight control. How could she know what the real Jeff was like? It was becoming obvious that her perception of Jon was not quite right.

"Ma! You coming?" Hal's voice drifted into her thoughts, bringing her back to the present. Worried about her driving alone after the incident the previous night, Hal had insisted on picking her up on their way in. Maggie had been too tired to argue. She could relax in the back seat with the boys while Hal handled the weekend traffic.

It was a beautiful evening. The air was cool and fresh. Out at Hal's, the stars would be shining overhead, numerous shards of twinkling light, much like the shimmering bits of glass on the large chandelier on the Phantom set. Here in the city, it was difficult to see the night sky; there was too much reflection from the lights on the ground. Lights on the streets, in the buildings, in the parking lots.

As Hal negotiated the semibusy streets, and her grandsons debated their favorite part of the play, Maggie's mind wandered. Maybe that's what had driven Jon out of the city that night. Perhaps he'd just wanted to see the stars and had driven out to the part of the city he'd known as a boy. Maggie sighed. It was frustrating to admit, but they would probably never know. Jon was likely the only person who really knew what had taken him out to the desert that fateful night. And he wouldn't be telling anyone.

Chapter Seventeen

"Look at that." Maggie nudged Victoria with her elbow and nodded toward the newest arrival. The Bee women sat together for Jonathan's funeral, lined up in the pew behind Carmen. A tall, lean man in a western-style suit had just entered the church, pausing to look around. He had thick salt-and-pepper hair and the leathery brown skin of someone who spent many hours in the sun.

"Who is he?" Victoria whispered.

"He's a neighbor of Hal's. Was a neighbor of ours from the time Harry and I moved in. He's a tough old geezer, kind of a loner."

"He looks like a gentleman rancher," Victoria observed.

"That's what's so odd. I've never seen him look so good." Maggie glanced again at his tan suit. The quality was good, the cut well suited to Harley. He'd shaved and had a haircut too.

"He's a character—I always thought he must be like the original settlers here in the valley. He has that independent streak; doesn't want anyone interfering with his life." Maggie looked him up and down once more, watching him make his way toward a pew at the side of the church. "I can hardly believe he's here, much less all dressed up and cleaned up. He usually looks like an old prospector who's been living in the desert for months. The last time I saw him he had at least a two-week growth of beard and that was just on Monday afternoon." Maggie's gaze moved down to his feet. "He even polished his boots."

"Funerals can bring out that side of people," Victoria suggested.

"Hmm. Maybe." *Or romance,* Maggie thought. But she remained silent then, as Father Bob came forward and the organ began the first notes of the opening hymn.

Afterward, Maggie and the other Bee members stood together in the courtyard, waiting to follow the hearse out to the graveyard. All of Maggie's sons had come, though Frank and Bobby left immediately after the service. Hal and Michael stood together, ready to get into Michael's car.

Anna dabbed at her eyes with a lace-trimmed hankie. "It's so sad when young people die."

"It's these dangerous times," Edie intoned. "Too much violence, too many guns."

"Oh, Edie." Louise was often short of patience where Edie was concerned. "He wasn't killed with a gun."

"Carjackers, probably." Edie was smugly satisfied with this conclusion.

Maggie was too busy watching Carmen and Harley to bother with Edie's theories. She was leaning over, ready to ask the others what they thought of the strange couple, when they were interrupted by the dark-suited young man from the mortuary. It was time to get in the car and line up for the trip to the cemetery.

At the graveside, Maggie continued to observe Carmen. She was in another role today, Maggie thought. The bereaved mother. Then Maggie scolded herself for being catty. Carmen *was* a bereaved mother after all. Maggie couldn't imagine losing one of her sons or of being able to get through the services with anything approaching grace. And that was what Carmen is doing, Maggie realized. Getting through it with grace.

Carmen wore a black suit, a beautifully styled garment that suited her small stature. Her hair was smartly coifed, her makeup perfect. Now, near the end of the ceremonies, most of the makeup had been removed by frequent wipes of a tissue.

But the thing that interested Maggie most was the way she leaned on Harley's arm. Fragile and pale, Carmen sagged against Harley, and he in turn looked down at her, supporting her with frequent touches of his hand on hers.

Maggie found herself scanning the others who had followed the hearse out to the grave site. Hal and Michael, of course. Carmen and Harley. The Quilting Bee. There were a few people from the old neighborhood. Winona Winthrop was there, looking incomplete without Samson at her side. A few others Maggie knew. And some earnest-looking young men and women who she thought must be journalists. She looked around the cemetery one last time. At least none of the local television stations had sent a cameraman.

The Bee gathered at Maggie's house afterward, standing in the dining room where a plethora of black and dark gray fabrics were spread over the table. At one end of the table, Maggie had set up her rotary cutter and mat. The pattern requirements were written carefully on a sheet of paper, copies available for each of the members.

"I brought my rotary cutter and mat, too," Louise told Maggie. She was carrying a large canvas tote. "I'll set it up on the kitchen table." She moved toward the kitchen, grabbing one of the instruction sheets as she went.

With the ease of people who had worked together for years, the women quickly set up an assembly line method of constructing the blocks, two cutting, two assembling, two sewing. Once the cutting was done, the two cutters became pressers. In no time at all, a stack of blocks sat at the end of the ironing board. By late afternoon, they had assembled and sewn over sixty blocks. Maggie took them into her bedroom and laid them side by side on her bed.

"They look good," Edie said.

Louise agreed. "It will be a very nice quilt."

"I'll make an appliqué block for the center—with his name on it. And some red roses, I think."

Clare looked them over, brushing her hand over the block closest to her. "I can't wait for Monday. Imagine meeting all the actors." She released a long sigh.

"It will be exciting," Anna agreed.

Maggie looked over the blocks with a critical eye, but could find nothing to object to. They were nice-looking blocks and would look even better when they surrounded the center block she visualized and with the plain white pieces filled with signatures.

Victoria began to gather up the blocks. "We'll help you press on the freezer paper before we go. They won't be used to writing on fabric, so they'll need the support the paper will give."

Louise had to leave to pick up her husband Vince from the golf course, but the others returned to the kitchen where they quickly cut the squares of freezer paper and pressed them to the back of the finished blocks.

"Let's have some tea," Maggie suggested, once all the work was completed. "I have some applesauce bread."

With all the sewing equipment put away, and tea and bread before them, the women settled down at the kitchen table.

Edie started right in, with a click of her tongue. "Did you see Carmen at the funeral this morning? Flirting with that man at her own son's funeral."

Anna looked shocked. "Oh, Edie, I don't think so. He was just trying to make her feel better comforting her. And it's not as if she's married or anything."

"Who was he, Maggie? Do you know?" Clare asked.

"He's Harley Stoner, a neighbor of Hal's. He's lived out that way forever, and he's quite a character," Maggie told them. "I ran into him out in the desert on Monday afternoon when I was taking my ride. He's the one who pointed out to me where Jon's body was found."

"Maggie said he cleaned up very well for the funeral," Victoria informed them.

Maggie nodded. "I'll say. When I first caught sight of him on Monday, I thought he might be a homeless man. He didn't look like much, tramping over the desert with his dog, unshaven, his clothes all rumpled."

"I thought he was a nice-looking man," Anna observed. "But I suppose if he wasn't all dressed up he might look like one of those old-timers you see in photographs of territorial Arizona. He has that look about the eyes that I imagine they had. Kind of a dreamy look, I suppose, looking ahead to those riches they hoped to find."

Maggie and the others were staring at Anna. It was one of the longest speeches Maggie had ever heard from her.

"That's very observant of you," Victoria told her. "I know just what you mean and you're right. A kind of distant vision. Mr. Stoner does have it. But if he tramps about in the desert as much as you seem to think, Maggie, might he have seen something that night that could give the police a clue as to who killed Jon?"

Maggie shook her head. "I doubt it. We talked about it that first day."

"Well, I still think one of the other actors is a logical choice," Clare said. "I can hardly wait to meet them on Monday."

"You're looking forward to eating barbecue with a murderer?"

Leave it to Edie to spoil their anticipation.

"Oh, dear. I hadn't thought of it that way." Clare's forehead wrinkled in concern.

Anna was beginning to look a little pale.

"Don't be silly," Maggie told them. "Edie, you're the one who's been insisting it must have been a carjacker. But the other actors were the last people to see Jonathan alive. They may be able to help us figure out what happened."

"We can establish a timetable," Victoria decided.

"Wouldn't the police have done that?" Anna inquired.

"It doesn't matter," Maggie said. "We'll make our own. It will be fun. And then we'll sew the blocks together and finish up the quilt with a few well-placed appliqué roses. Red ones."

While the others exclaimed over how perfect that would be, Maggie gathered together what she needed for the center block. Edie was very good at writing on the blocks, so while Maggie sketched out her idea for the roses, Edie went to work on the lettering. By the time the others left, Maggie had all the pieces of the center block cut, pinned, and ready to sew.

Chapter Eighteen

Maggie enjoyed her Sunday brunches with Hal and his family. It was their tradition, carried over from the days when the boys were young, to attend the 10:00 mass at St. Rose, then return to the house for a hearty brunch with the whole family. Hal and his wife continued the tradition when Harry died and Maggie turned the ranch over to them. Though there were now other churches closer to the ranch, they still drove down to St. Rose. Harry and Maggie had been married there, as had Hal and Sara, Frank and April, and Bobby and Merrie. Not all the boys and their families made the Sunday brunch every week, but Michael could usually be counted on.

This week, everyone was there. Because of the beautiful weather, they were seated at picnic tables on the patio. Maggie and Sara were still standing, checking on the food, making sure everyone had all they needed. Hal was speaking to his brothers.

"Harley came to see me again, about buying that piece of property."

Maggie, standing at the children's table, turned swiftly, the serving spoon in her hand littering the air with droplets of liquid from the fruit salad. "Does he have the money?"

Hal shook his head. "No."

Sara glanced around one last time and took her place beside Hal. "But why does Harley want it?" she asked, reaching for the platter of French toast. "He's getting on in years. What will he do with it?"

Frank agreed. "I can't believe he'd be able to work a larger ranch. And he doesn't have any children."

Bobby nodded. "It's hard to believe he can work the place he has now."

Hal shrugged. Without being asked, he passed the maple syrup to his wife, following up with the platter of sausages and bacon. "He manages fine. But I think he just likes to acquire land. Keep adding to his place, making it bigger and better."

Maggie nodded. "Southerners are often like that."

"Funny," Michael said. "I always thought Harley was local. He's always struck me as the original Arizona type—strong, independent. Kind of a redneck. It's easy to picture him prospecting in the mountains."

Maggie exchanged a look with Hal. This sounded remarkably like the conversation they had had on Thursday afternoon. "Oh, he used to."

The others looked at Maggie in surprise. She took the platter of meat from Sara and put two pieces of bacon on her plate. "When we first met him he used to do some prospecting. We all moved out here about the same time, you know. Harley and his wife. Your dad and I. Winona and Carl."

"Harley had a wife?" Michael asked the question, but the others were just as surprised.

"Oh, yes. Her name was Patsy. She was a lovely woman. Very sweet. Didn't like the desert. She was from Prescott and very genteel. Definitely a city girl, or a small-town one. She didn't like the loneliness. This area was far from everywhere back in those days, and going into Scottsdale for the shopping was a big deal. And then Harley was always heading off somewhere hoping to make a fortune, leaving her alone at the ranch." Maggie paused to take a bite of her breakfast, remembering the lovely, petite young woman. She'd been totally unsuited for life on a deserted ranch.

"She made exquisite quilts," she went on. "She's the one who got me started doing appliqué. Before that I just used to piece." Maggie wondered if the boys remembered any of the quilts she had made for them in those days of their youth. Patsy had given her many of the patterns: zoo animals, cars and trucks, and Overall Sam.

"Well, Mom," Michael said. "Don't stop now. Tell us more."

"Yes." Sara laughed. "I'm trying real hard to picture Harley with a pretty little city girl who did exquisite needlework."

Maggie wanted to laugh with her, but the actual story was too sad. She and Patsy had been friends and she had ached for the woman. "It might have worked if they'd had a child. She wanted a baby so bad. It was right after you were born, Frank, that she left. I think it was too much for her seeing my two boys all the time. She finally moved back home and filed for divorce." Maggie stopped long enough to sip her coffee. "Harley was always a bit odd, but he got even worse after that."

"What a lovely, romantic story," Merrie exclaimed. "What a shame it ended so sadly."

"How on earth did the two of them ever get together?" Sara asked.

"Apparently, their families knew one another back in Mississippi. Harley went up to visit when he first moved here. He was a nice-looking man in his young days, and very polite. She said it was love at first sight on both their parts, but her family made them wait until Harley had established himself—bought the property out here, built the house, that sort of thing. Then they got married."

"I wonder why they didn't settle in Prescott, so she could be near her family?" Sara was so interested in the story of Harley's ill-fated marriage that her food sat almost untouched on her plate.

"She would have liked that." Maggie pushed her plate aside and topped off her coffee. All this reminiscing didn't seem to enhance her appetite. "Living near her family probably would have helped their marriage. But Harley always did like the desert, and I can't see him living anywhere else. They were just oil and water, those two."

"Wait a minute." Michael's voice broke through the increasing noise from the children's table. "You said you all moved out here at about the same time. As newlyweds. Do you mean that Harley and Dad were about the same age?" Michael's incredulousness at the idea was apparent in his voice.

"Oh, yes. They were very close in age, and they got on real well. They liked to talk about horses, and they'd go hunting together. Things cooled off some when Patsy left and Harley began to turn into a recluse, but your dad always liked him, and they were still friends. We tried to keep up with him, but he turned down our invitations to dinners and get-togethers after Patsy left. I don't know if he was embarrassed or ashamed. He aged after that, too. He looks eighty but he's barely old enough for Social Security."

None of the others could believe that Harley Stoner and their father were contemporaries.

"Now that I think about it . . ." Maggie's voice turned thoughtful. "Harley did become more sociable after a while. And I think it was right about the time you were born, Michael. Right after Carmen and Ed Hunter moved into the neighborhood."

"I noticed them at the funeral," Michael said. "Harley looked like a million. I think he likes her."

A crash and a squeal followed by girlish sobs, effectively ended the brunch. April and Maggie rushed over to the children's table to check on Megan, Sara close behind. The boys had been fooling around and managed to spill a half-filled glass of orange juice into Megan's lap. As April wiped up her daughter, the adults began the cleanup process. The two boys ran off to play.

"So, Michael . . . we saw you leave with the actress the other night." Frank couldn't resist teasing his brother.

Michael brushed his brother off with a shrug. "She's nice. And she likes *'Star Trek.'* "

His brothers groaned.

Bobby laughed. "Obviously a match made in heaven."

"On a more serious note," Hal began. "What's happening with the investigation into Jon's death? Are you going to be arresting anyone sometime soon?"

Maggie began to pay attention. She sat on a picnic bench with her arm around a still aggrieved Megan, an ideal spot from which to eavesdrop on her sons' conversation.

"Doesn't look like there will be an arrest soon, no." Michael shook his head, his frustration evident. "Of course, it's not my case, but I've been trying to follow the investigation just because he was my friend. And so far things seem to be stalled."

"Why hasn't his car turned up?" Maggie asked.

"That's the sixty-four-thousand-dollar question."

Chapter Nineteen

Victoria drove to St. Rose on Monday morning. Maggie met her in the carport, feeling rested for the first time in a week.

Victoria, too, looked bright and alert. "Can you believe it's only been a week since we heard about Jonathan?"

It was the same thing the others were saying when they arrived at the church. The Grandmother's Fan quilt would be done in a few days; at this point they would usually be discussing what top they would quilt next and debating on the best quilting design to use. But today all the talk was once again about Jonathan Hunter.

Until Carmen appeared in their doorway around 10:00.

Maggie jumped up from her chair to welcome her. "Carmen! How nice to see you here again. Did we give you the quilting bug?"

The others chimed in their own welcomes and Maggie was glad to see that Carmen was smiling and friendly. Although she wouldn't have been able to fault her for being downhearted and depressed, her current mood was so much easier on those around her.

"Oh, I'm not staying." To Maggie's surprise, a blush tinted Carmen's cheeks. "I'm having lunch with Harley Stoner." Her eyes sought Maggie's. "I know you remember him, Maggie. It was so nice of him to come to the funeral."

"He must have been that nice-looking man in the western suit," Anna said.

"Yes, that's Harley." Carmen's lashes fluttered to her cheeks as she mentioned her former neighbor. "He'd always been very nice to Jonathan and me, but I was so surprised to see him at the church. I hadn't really expected anyone but you nice ladies," she added. "That was really why I stopped by today. I wanted to thank you all for coming to the funeral. I really appreciated having you there."

Carmen approached Maggie and leaned over so that she could give her a hug. Maggie found herself enveloped in a cloud of rose-scented air.

"I especially wanted to thank you and your sons, Maggie. I was very touched to have them come and say their farewells to Jon. He loved all your sons, not just Michael, and always talked about the good times they all had playing together."

Feeling that the thanks had run on long enough, Maggie jumped up from her chair.

"I'm glad you're here, Carmen. We made up the memory quilt blocks on Saturday afternoon, you know. I have them with me. Would you like to see them?"

"Oh, I'd love to."

Carmen followed Maggie over to the table at one side of the room where she'd left the bag holding the blocks. The other Bee members also got up and gathered at the table, declaring themselves ready for a break.

Maggie removed the blocks from her tote bag, arranging them carefully on the table around the larger center block. She'd worked on the roses all Saturday and Sunday night in order to get them done. The crisp blocks in deep blacks and shades of gray twisted around the center block with its red roses and Jonathan's name inscribed in Edie's best calligraphy. Maggie frowned at them. "Of course, the signatures will be in the white spaces," she told Carmen.

"It needs a little more color," Louise observed, staring at the blocks with a frown of her own. "After you sew them together, you should add a narrow red border, then another wider one in black."

Maggie nodded.

"Remember, Maggie said she would add a few more roses as well," Victoria reminded them.

"That will help." Louise continued to stare at the blocks, then finally nodded her approval. "Yes, that will work. Otherwise the black, white, and gray are just too monotone."

A quiet voice interrupted. "I think it's lovely."

The women had almost forgotten Carmen, the intended recipient, in their analytical observation of the blocks. Now they all turned toward her, touched to see the tears in her eyes.

"This is so special of you, creating this wonderful quilt for me. I'll never forget how nice you all were. How can I ever thank you?" She began rummaging in her handbag for a tissue, but by the time she found one, she'd managed to blink back her tears. Still, she stood at the table, holding the crumpled tissue in her hand, her lashes damp and heavy, looking at the women around her.

Victoria put her arm around Carmen. "No thanks are necessary. We wanted to do it."

Once again, Maggie broke off the heavy moment. "I'll sew them together after the party this evening and then do borders and some appliqué roses. I'll quilt it by machine. I'm afraid it will be a while yet before you can have it."

"It doesn't matter. You're going to all this trouble for me. And I think I told you before that I had the apartment here for another two weeks."

Clare, standing beside Carmen, nudged her with her elbow and smiled. "It will give you time for more luncheons with that old neighbor of yours."

"And dinners," Edie added.

Carmen's cheeks brightened once more. Maggie couldn't believe that a fifty-year-old woman could blush. But here was the proof that it could indeed happen. She'd done it twice now.

"Harley was a good neighbor and very nice to Jonathan and me."

Maggie realized it was the second time she'd said this. She also remembered Harley's questions to her about Carmen and the way he seemed to be more animated when he spoke of her. Nevertheless, it was hard to think of Harley having a romance.

"I still can't believe the old curmudgeon asked you out on a date. I wonder if this is a first for him?"

Carmen defended her friend. "Oh, he isn't so bad. I think he's kind of shy."

Maggie tried not to laugh at this observation. Carmen didn't seem to notice her facial contortions, though Victoria did and began steering the others back to the quilt frame. Carmen continued to speak, unaware of the movements around her. "Harley was such a big help to Jon and me after Ed disappeared. I don't know what I would have done without him."

Maggie noticed the way Carmen referred to Ed's desertion as a "disappearance." Poor Carmen still couldn't admit that the man had just taken off. "If I remember correctly, Harley hated Ed."

Carmen hedged. "Well, he and Ed didn't get along."

"Did he keep in touch? With you I mean," Maggie clarified.

"Oh, he did. For a while. But, you know, things were hard for me at first." Carmen dropped her head, her eyes on the floor. "I was embarrassed that I was making such a mess of my life. Then when things got better, I was embarrassed about all the times I'd ignored his letters."

"Well, well." Maggie began gathering up the quilt blocks, stacking them carefully to return to her tote. "Sounds like we have a little romance going here."

Carmen blushed once more. "Oh, I think it's just two old friends getting together. He's a bit older than me, you know."

Maggie dismissed that with a wave of her hand. "That doesn't mean anything. Nowadays it doesn't matter if the *woman* is older. Or taller."

"That's right," Louise agreed. The others had returned to their quilting but they continued to monitor the conversation.

"I do like a tall man, though," Clare admitted. "How tall is Harley? He looked over six feet at church, but he had boots on and that adds a little."

Carmen shrugged. "I'm not good at estimating heights. But he's quite a bit taller than me. He must be over six feet. He's a large man, much bigger than Ed ever was. Or Jonathan," she added more quietly.

"Jonathan wasn't tall?" Clare asked.

Maggie shook her head. "It's surprising how many actors aren't tall. They always seem so large in movies and on television. Jonathan had such a marvelous stage presence, you expected him to be very tall. But he wasn't, was he?"

Pride shone from Carmen's face. "No. He was five-eleven, but he always seemed much taller. It was because he was so alive—as you said, he had so much stage presence." The memories caused Carmen to choke on a sob. The realization that he was no longer alive sent her digging in her purse for a tissue, forgetting that she already clutched one in her hand.

Concerned, the Quilting Bee ladies hurried to her side. Clare led her to a chair, while Anna rushed out to the kitchen for a cup of tea.

Soon she was seated beside them, sipping from a steaming mug.

"Now you just sit there and relax for a few minutes. You want to look fresh when you meet Harley," Victoria told her.

Mention of Harley had an amazing effect on Carmen. She quickly calmed down, her facial muscles relaxing into an expression of smooth calm. Clare told them how she'd met her husband, and how his height had been one of the first things she'd noticed about him. Louise picked up with a tale about her daughter and a man she'd once dated who was at least five inches shorter.

By the time Carmen looked at her watch and announced she had to go, they were all laughing together and having a good time.

Chapter Twenty

Multiple shades of purple, pink, and orange painted the desert sky as the sun sank behind the mountains to the west. In Hal's backyard, floodlights broke through the rosy light of the dying day and lent an artificial brightness to the green grass and the casual clothes of the partygoers.

The party for the cast members was going well. Platters of barbecued beef and chicken were disappearing as quickly as they appeared on the tables. Bowls of baked beans, potato and fruit salads, chips and salsa, trays of fresh vegetables—nothing seemed unpopular with the out-of-town guests. Given how thin most of them were, the actors had surprisingly good appetites.

"This is so great of you," Judy told Maggie, talking around the melon ball she'd just bitten into. "It's been so long since I had home-cooked food, I'd forgotten how good it is. Though I probably won't fit into my costumes tomorrow night," she added with a groan.

Michael had appeared beside her, a fresh platter of steaming chicken in his hands. "You look like you could use a good meal. How can just one make a difference?"

Judy rolled her eyes and sent Maggie a woman-to-woman look that Maggie understood immediately. *"Men just don't understand,"* it said. To Michael, however, she merely replied, "You wouldn't believe how quickly a costume can get too small."

But Maggie noticed that she helped herself to another drumstick anyway, before strolling off with Michael. Were the two of them getting to be friends? Did they share more than an interest in a TV show? Or was Maggie just trying to read something into it because she liked Judy so much?

Shrugging at her inability to answer that question, Maggie picked up an empty salad bowl and headed for the kitchen. She met Sara there, busy replenishing trays of cruditees from the plastic bags they'd filled earlier.

"I have to thank you again for letting me impose on you like this," Maggie told her. They had spent most of the afternoon together preparing the salads and vegetables, but Maggie still felt the need to thank her daughter-in-law. They had a good relationship and Maggie wanted to keep it that way. "This was a big group to spring on you at the last minute."

Sara shrugged off Maggie's thanks. "It's a pleasure. This place is as much yours as it is mine. Besides, the boys and I are having a wonderful time."

Maggie laughed. "*Everyone* is having a wonderful time."

They looked out the open arcadia doors. A lazy evening breeze wafted inside, cooling the kitchen and bringing the appetizing aroma of barbecue with it. The three picnic tables outside had been augmented by a number of borrowed tables of various sizes and all of them were filled. Lawn and pool chairs strung about the yard were also full. The cast and crew had turned out in strength.

The members of the St. Rose Quilting Bee were scattered among the guests, helping the actors with their quilt blocks. Also, they saw that the finished blocks were well protected from salsa, dip, and barbecue sauce.

At the table where Jeff Manchester and Kevin Czar sat, Jason and Joshua were speaking animatedly. The actors were replying with smiles, hand gestures, and equal animation. Lydia and some of the other dancers were grouped around Anna and Louise, who were giving them tips on how to write on fabric.

Music floated out over the yard from a boom box on the patio, yet the noise level was high enough to almost drown out the strains of Randy Travis. Everyone was indeed having a good time.

Maggie was enjoying herself, too, she realized, as she glanced once more around the yard. It had been a long time since she'd had a party. And although she was tired form the preparations, she was still happy to be there. It was a pleasant kind of tiredness.

Still standing in the doorway, observing the party outside, Maggie saw Carmen walking toward her, her hands full of dirty paper plates. To Sara's surprise, but not Maggie's, Carmen had arrived with Harley in tow. He'd hovered at her side all evening, reminding Maggie of a mother bear protecting a cub. Maggie wondered if he thought one of the people in the yard had killed Jon. Is that why he seemed afraid to leave Carmen's side? Unbidden, her eyes moved to the table where Jeff and Kevin sat.

Carmen reached the patio and smiled at Maggie. Harley, her shadow this evening, remained a few steps behind her.

"This is so nice of you. Of you both," she added, acknowledging Sara with a nod as she deposited the used cups and plates in a trash can. Dusting her hands off, she moved into the kitchen. Harley stayed on the patio but kept his eyes on Carmen. Maggie wondered if he was afraid to insinuate himself into what he considered a "woman's area."

"This is the best wake a person could have," Carmen continued. "I'm sure Jonathan is proud to know his friends are here remembering him, enjoying themselves, creating something special. He was such a creative person himself that I know this would appeal to him."

Maggie couldn't help wondering at Carmen's mercurial nature. Just a few days ago she had indicated that none of the cast were true friends of Jon's.

She put her arm around Carmen's shoulders. "We're glad to do it. This quilt will be something you'll have to help you remember him and all his friends. It will be a comfort."

Carmen nodded. Tears filled her eyes. "I don't know how I would have managed without friends like you." She looked at Maggie and Sara, then back outside at Harley. Her dark eyes softened and she smiled.

Maggie exchanged a look with Victoria, who had just come in with some empty chip bowls to refill. Her eyebrows raised, she seemed to be asking, *"Is something going on here?"* Victoria glanced at Carmen and Harley, then answered Maggie's unspoken question with a shrug.

Carmen approached Maggie, gave her a hug, then did the same to Sara and Victoria. "I'm so grateful I hardly know what to say. But I"—she glanced shyly at Harley—"uh, we, have to be going. I don't want to cramp the young people's style by hanging around. They might not want to reminisce too much about Jon if his *mother* is right there." The special emphasis and her smile indicated the kind of things she imagined men might like to remember, but not in front of middle-aged matrons.

She moved out of the kitchen, took Harley's arm, and within minutes had made her farewells and was gone.

Outside, Jason and Joshua had finally left the *Phantom* actors in order to show some of the others the horses. The empty plates had been cleared away, and Anna and Clare sat beside Jeff and Kevin, assisting the two men with their blocks.

"You have to be careful or the pen will catch in the threads of the fabric," Clare warned. She offered them each a sample piece of the white fabric to practice on. "You have to have a light touch."

"I can do that." Jeff laughed. He was a fine-looking man, with dancing blue eyes and a generous mouth.

Anna was in heaven, helping them with their contributions to the memory quilt. She hoped her little grandson would be as nice as these two gentlemen one day. No matter what Clare thought, she just couldn't imagine either of them killing poor Jonathan Hunter. She watched Jeff's long artist's fingers as he finished his practice signature and began on the block itself. "I'll bet you play the piano."

Concentrating on what he was doing, Jeff answered distractedly. "I used to." he finished his signature and handed over the block.

"Oh, that's so clever," Anna exclaimed, taking the finished block and holding it out before her to examine it. "I love the little mask you drew on there." She sighed as she turned it for Clare to see before adding it to the stack on the table. Beside his name, Jeff had sketched a simple but unmistakable Phantom mask.

"I saw you perform the other night, and you were wonderful." Anna smiled shyly at Jeff. "My son-in-law got tickets for us."

"Thank you." His blue eyes seemed to darken with emotion as he answered her. "I wish I had been filling in for any other reason, though."

Kevin, the second understudy, completed his work and handed the fabric to Anna. Once again she cried out in pleasure. "Oh. And you drew a rose. You're all so wonderfully talented. You sing and act and draw . . ."

The two men laughed. "Anna, you're welcome to visit us anytime," Jeff told her, putting his arm around her shoulders in a casual hug.

"Yes," seconded Kevin. "What a pleasure you are to have around. I think we should make you ladies our official Phoenix area fan club."

Clare laughed too as she capped the fabric pens they had been using and pushed them to one side. But she sobered abruptly. "How did you feel about Jonathan? Really."

Jeff blinked at her in surprise, his lips pulling down into a frown. A quick look of anger or frustration passed quickly over his face and was just as quickly gone. But Kevin answered freely. "He was an okay guy."

"Yeah," agreed Jeff. His face was schooled into a look of perfect decorum, with just enough sadness to be appropriate at a wake. "He was no better or worse than anyone else in this business. That 'he was a great guy' stuff is for the newspapers. He lost his temper sometimes, you know, and sometimes he helped somebody out. He was just an ordinary guy."

"Did you get to do the Phantom role much?" Clare still liked the idea of the understudy as villain. And Jeff was a complicated guy who she felt was masking his true feelings.

"Oh, yeah. We both got to go on quite often. It's a demanding part and there are a lot of performances in a week. We always got to do the part a time or two in each city. Sometimes more."

"That's right. Jon had a head cold in Denver and we shared the performances for over a week," Jeff said.

Kevin nodded. "He was feeling dizzy from the congestion and couldn't climb up into the sets because of the danger of falling."

"How interesting." *How disappointing,* Clare thought. It seemed her excellent theory had no foundation after all. Though that didn't explain Jeff's almost angry look when she'd asked about Jon. Then another thought occurred to her. "Who will get the part now?"

"They'll probably send in someone."

Kevin nodded his agreement.

"You mean they won't give it to one of you?" Anna's voice reflected her feeling that this was a great injustice.

Again that flash of anger, quickly hidden. "It's possible, but that isn't the way it's usually done," Jeff told her.

"Well, I think one of you deserves the part." Amid their smiling thank-yous, Anna rose from her chair. "It was so nice meeting you. I can't wait to tell my grandchildren."

Clare was consulting a list they'd made of all the major characters in the play. "Let's see . . . Almost everyone has signed a block now. But we still need Susanne Koralski, Tanya Kessler, and Roman Maggiore."

"I don't see Tanya," Jeff said, looking around the yard. "But I'm sure she's here. I saw her earlier. And Roman is over by the pool with the dancers."

Anna turned to look. "That handsome young man with the long dark hair?"

"That's right. But I don't think Susanne is here," Kevin said. "If she was she'd be over there with Roman. She has family in this area, and she usually spends her time off with them."

Maggie passed by their table just in time to hear this last. Things were beginning to wind down. Sara had shooed her out of her kitchen, and she couldn't resist coming out to see the finished quilt blocks. Now she stopped, her hands on a finished block, to process what had just been said.

"Is that Tanya you're talking about? She has family here?"

"No, Susanne does," Kevin replied. "In fact, I think she's staying with someone local during the run of the show. I seem to remember her saying how nice it was to have a real home to go back to every night instead of a hotel room."

"How interesting." Maggie filed away that piece of information, then proceeded to compliment the men on their autographed blocks. "I'm so glad you did unique little things like drawing the mask or the rosebud. It will make the quilt very special."

While Clare told the actors she would take a picture of the finished quilt to send them, Maggie moved toward the other side of the yard. It was too early for roses, but looking at the little drawings, Maggie felt drawn to the rose garden.

The rose garden was a mass of awakening plants, the new leaves a mixture of deep green and tender red. The rain earlier this year which had turned the mountains behind them green, had kept the temperatures low, so that the rose bushes didn't regenerate as early as they sometimes did. But even without the fragrant blooms, the small garden had drawn another person to its secluded preserve. Shielded from the main part of the yard by the house, the rose garden was an L-shaped area between a back room of the house and the long wall of the garage. Cloaked in shadow, even as the characters often were in their stage play, a slender jeans-clad figure stood at the angle of the L, as fragile and graceful as the newly awakened rose bushes. In the dimness of the night, Maggie could not tell if the figure was male or female. Longish hair was pulled back into a ponytail, but Maggie knew that hair length was no longer an indication of gender.

Maggie approached quietly, unwilling to break the mood that hung over the little garden as an oasis of peace in the midst of the noisy party.

"I've always liked this spot," Maggie confided. Her voice was low, intimate, almost reverent, but the person standing there was startled enough to jump. Turning toward Maggie, her eyes wide in the dim light, Maggie realized that the person standing there was the heretofore elusive Tanya.

Maggie kept her voice soft and intimate. "Jon liked this place, too. I'd work out here in the afternoons while he and my sons played in the yard. There was a sandbox right over there." Maggie nodded toward a towering acacia tree. "But lots of times he would come over and watch me. Ask what I was doing and why. He liked the roses; he would ask me their names, and he'd remember them. Later he'd call the blooms by name when he talked to me about them."

There was a long sigh from Tanya, and a gentle shake of her head. "Doesn't sound much like the Jon I knew. How old was he then?"

Her speaking voice was soft and musical, and Maggie thought she'd give the world to hear her sing, right now, right here. "He was six or seven, I suppose. But people do change. Tell me what he was like as an adult. I've talked to Carmen, but it's hard to believe everything she says. I think she's idealized him as the perfect son right now."

"The perfect son. That's a laugh." Tanya chuckled but it was not a particularly happy sound. "He never wanted her around. Though sometimes he did decide to invite her to a show and then he would play the role of the perfect son." She made a noise in her throat that was neither chuckle nor sob. "If Jon was the perfect anything, it was an egotist." She gave a grim laugh. "Actually he was the perfect Phantom. Not that he would have killed anyone. But he wanted what he wanted and he didn't let anyone get in his way."

"He doesn't sound like someone to admire."

"And you're wondering what I saw in him?" Tanya fingered a smooth new leaf, still red in its infancy. "He could be charming. And boyish. He could be a lot of fun. And don't ever forget that Jonathan Hunter was a wonderful actor. He would have gone places. It was just a matter of time until he would have been starring on Broadway."

"And taken you with him?"

Tanya shrugged. "Maybe." The thin shoulders straightened under the fabric of her shirt. "I'm a good actress."

"Of course you are. I saw you and Jonathan perform last week. You have a wonderful voice." Maggie touched a tight bud. Even if the light was better, there would be nothing but green there. "Carmen seems to think that you and Jon were practically engaged."

Tanya gave another brittle laugh. "Jon wasn't ready to settle down. He liked having his personal space, but mostly he wanted the freedom to see whoever he wanted. Loyalty was not a big part of Jon's character."

"It must have been difficult to maintain a relationship with him."

Tanya shrugged. "We both knew it wouldn't last. And he could be mean when he wanted to be. But I did like him most of the time."

"It must be hard for you now, with him dead, and you the chief suspect."

Michael's voice startled both women. Tanya turned on her heel, her hair flying out behind her. Maggie clutched at her chest and scolded her son.

"Heavens, Michael. Are you trying to give me a heart attack?"

Michael tried to look apologetic, but Maggie knew he wasn't too sorry. It was the cop in him. He must have seen her come this way and followed. She wondered how much of the conversation he'd heard.

"This is my son Michael," Maggie finally said. "Tanya Kessler. Judy has been filling in for her this week."

"Oh, do you know Judy?"

Tanya may have hoped to change the direction of the conversation, but if that was the case, she'd misjudged Michael.

"We've just recently met," Michael told her. "I had heard that you and Jon were practically engaged. Is that why you were unable to go on all week?"

"It was the first night. I was upset about Jon, and even more upset about all the questions from the police. But then I caught a cold and couldn't sing. And we weren't practically engaged. Jon wasn't the type for a commitment."

"I thought maybe that was why he wanted to buy that land from my brother. You know, so he could settle down."

Tanya laughed. "Jon? Settle down? Surely you jest."

It was Michael's turn to shrug. "We were best friends when we were kids. But we'd lost touch over the years. You know how it is. A card at Christmas. A phone call now and then. He had indicated there was something he wanted to tell me though."

Tanya's lips tightened and her eyes took on a sorrowful cast. She drew her hands away from the rose bush as though afraid that her restless fingers would be punctured by a thorn. "I knew him before. We'd done a short run of *Chorus Line* together. He'd changed. Getting the lead in a big show went to his head, I think."

Maggie couldn't resist a comment. "Everyone said he was such a nice guy." It drew the annoyed look she expected from Michael.

Tanya's voice was free of emotion. If she had truly loved him at some point, it must have been over before his death. "He was nice when it paid to be nice."

"You sound like you didn't care much for him. Yet you were dating, and the others seemed to think it was pretty serious."

Again the shrug. "You have to do something in these strange cities. We're here for six weeks." Tanya shoved her hands into her pockets and hunched her shoulders. "It's nice to have a date for dinner and drinks. Maybe go dancing, or play miniature golf. We did that one afternoon. It was fun."

"I heard you left with him the night he was killed. From the restaurant."

Maggie was surprised to say the least. Michael hadn't said anything to her about that. But Tanya seemed equally surprised. Her head flew up, her eyes searching his face.

"You heard wrong."

Maggie thought she saw a trace of Carlotta's haughtiness in her expression.

"I left with Jeff." She took her hands out of her pockets and straightened her back. "Excuse me. I have to get back to the others."

Michael and Maggie watched her leave, thoughtful looks on both their faces.

"You made that up, didn't you?" Maggie's voice scolded him. "About her leaving with Jon."

Michael shrugged, unrepentant. "I wanted to see her reaction."

"So . . . do you think she did it?"

But to Maggie's frustration, Michael didn't answer. He murmured something about seeing Judy home and left the rose garden.

Maggie remained where she was, her mind going back over everything that was said. She was so intent on solving the puzzle of Jon's death that she didn't even register Michael's mention of Judy.

The rose garden worked its usual magic on her, eventually bringing an inner peace. The sound of the water as it fell from layer to layer in the fountain had a relaxing effect that made her eyelids droop. The night air was rapidly cooling, and Maggie was beginning to feel the cold. With a little shiver, she started back toward the house. Maybe going over everything with the Quilting Bee in the morning would help her sort through all she had learned.

Chapter Twenty-one

The next morning the Quilting Bee buzzed with talk of the memory quilt party.

"I just can't believe how nice all the actors were," Anna said. "Just like normal people."

There were a few laughs at this, much to Anna's surprise.

"Yes," Maggie agreed. "Even my grandsons were impressed by them. And they're the kind of boys who would normally make fun of a singing actor."

Some of the others nodded. They had grandchildren, too, or remembered how their own sons had felt.

Maggie nodded. "I'm so glad we took them all to the play. They really enjoyed it, and of course seeing the Phantom character was exciting for them."

"Little boys love a scary character," Clare agreed. "And the Phantom is scaring people and killing them. Kidnapping them. Very exciting."

"And there are good special effects," Maggie reminded them. "Joshua loved the scene in the graveyard where he throws sparks at Christine and Raoul."

"What a shame we didn't get to meet Susanne Koralski," Anna said. "She's the only one of the major characters who didn't sign a block for the quilt."

Clare sighed. "I still like my theory about the understudy. But now that I've met Jeff and Kevin, it is hard to believe either of them killed anyone."

Edie snorted. She had decided not to attend the barbecue, as she had a late appointment with the eye doctor. With her eyes sensitive from the eyedrops, she felt she'd better stay at home. Even at the best of times, she didn't like to drive at night.

"What do I keep telling you?" she said now. "You can't believe anything you see with those actors. That's their business. They're supposed to make you see what they want you to see."

Maggie was silent, but more and more she believed Edie might be right.

"There was something about Jeff, though," Clare began. "Nothing definite, just a feeling I had that he wasn't being entirely truthful in his statements about Jon."

"Are you sure you're not just imagining it because you favor him for the chief suspect?" Anna asked.

Maggie sent an understanding look across the frame to Clare. "I know just what you mean. It's this look he gets, but he covers it quickly."

Clare nodded. "That's it exactly. He says he didn't mind being the understudy, but I can't help thinking he's happier being the star."

Edie's laugh sounded closer to a snort. "Of course he would be."

"I think she just means that he's not being truthful," Victoria suggested.

They all mulled this over for a minute or two while they stitched.

"I finally got to talk to Tanya Kessler last night." Maggie's voice dropped into the quiet room, pulling their thoughts away from the handsome understudy. "And I also have an idea where Jon's missing car might be."

There were a few exclamations of surprise.

"Maggie!" Victoria looked at her friend in dismay. "Did you tell Michael about this?"

"Don't be silly. Of course not. I don't know after all. I'm going to try to find out this evening, after the show. All I have right now is a theory."

"Well, are you going to tell us your theory?" Louise held her needle poised above the quilt top waiting for the answer to her question.

Maggie frowned but apparently decided it was all right to tell them. "I found out last night that one of the cast members has relatives here in town." She looked at Anna and Clare. "That's why Susanne Koralski wasn't there. You were there when Jeff and Kevin mentioned it, remember? They said she wasn't there because she spent her free time with her relatives."

"That's right." Clare inserted her needle but didn't continue the stitch. She was too excited by this new idea to take the care necessary for the tiny stitches. "So you think she's got his car hidden at some relative's house? Why, then, she must have done it."

"Oh, Maggie." Anna was visibly upset. "You'd better be careful. If she's the one who killed him, you might be in danger."

"I'm not going to worry until I see her." Maggie tried to sound brave, but their concern was beginning to make her nervous. "The papers said Jon was killed by a blow to the head. What I read seemed to indicate the killer used a rock or something like that, picked up in the desert. Carmen said Jon was five-foot-eleven. That means it would take a tall woman to hit him with a rock and kill him. I saw Susanne at the theater last week and she's rather petite."

Louise thought this over. "I don't know. You'd better not take any chances, Maggie. That theory of a tall killer sounds good, but you'd have to see the autopsy records to be absolutely sure. The blow could have come from below, for instance. Or Jon could have been seated or bending over."

"Or he could have fallen and hit his head." Victoria's quiet voice entered a theory of her own.

"But that wouldn't be murder," Maggie insisted. "And all along, the police have been calling this a homicide.

So the evidence must point to him having been deliberately killed by someone."

"But what did his girlfriend have to say? Didn't you say you talked to Tanya Kessler last night?" Anna asked.

"That was a very interesting conversation," Maggie admitted. She continued to set her stitches as she told them about the conversation she'd had with Tanya and how Michael had shown up.

"So she denied being the last to see him." Victoria finished off her thread and reached for the scissors.

"She left with Jeff." Clare's excitement showed. "The understudy and the girlfriend. They could have done it together!"

This suggestion caused some noisy discussion.

"I'd like to see her again," Maggie finally said, continuing to stitch down the blade of a fan. "She's quite tall—at least five-nine, maybe five-ten. And I'm sure there was something she wasn't saying. . . ."

"Oh, dear. You'd better be careful, Maggie."

Anna appeared very concerned for her and Maggie felt touched. Maggie smiled reassuringly. "Don't worry, Anna. All I'm doing is visiting with a few friends."

Chapter Twenty-two

Late that night, as Maggie settled into bed, she remembered her words to Anna. Just visiting with a few friends indeed. Friends who were mixed up with lies and coverups, and just possibly murder.

The evening had started off as usual. She and Victoria arrived at the theater at 6:30 to stuff programs. There were less changes that evening. Tanya returned to her role as Carlotta, moving Judy back into her previous parts in the chorus. Susanne, who had missed her last performance, was appearing as Christine once again.

After the show, Victoria and Maggie walked the now-familiar path to the stage door. The orchestra members were already leaving when they arrived. The black-clad musicians smiled greetings to the two women they'd seen so often in the past week. A couple called out thanks for the barbecue.

To Maggie's surprise, Tanya was one of the first cast members to appear. Huddled in a jacket, with a baseball cap pulled low over her brow, Maggie thought she must be trying to escape autograph hunters. She asked Victoria to watch for Susanne and not to let her get away before she returned. Then she fell in step beside Tanya as she headed around the building.

"Tanya." She kept her voice low so as not to attract any of the autograph hunters. There were very few this evening, perhaps because the temperature had dropped and it was cold outside. But Tanya seemed to be trying to avoid fans, so Maggie didn't want to call attention to her.

Tanya barely glanced at her. "What do *you* want?" She continued to follow the path alongside the building.

"I think there was something you forgot to mention last night. About your relationship with Jon."

"Oh, yeah? What was that?"

"He'd broken it off, hadn't he?"

Tanya stopped abruptly and turned to Maggie. "Who *are* you, anyway?"

"I told you last night. I knew Jon when he was a child."

"Oh, yeah. I remember. The sweet little kid." The light was dim and the cap shaded her face, but Maggie knew there was a sneer on her pretty face.

Maggie kept her voice soft. "He *was* a sweet child. Quiet and very polite. My older boys used to tease him about it."

"Sweet and polite, huh?" She pushed her hands into the pockets of her jeans and leaned forward on the balls of her feet. "Of course the Phantom can be sweet and polite, too." A strange smile twisted her lips. "And in the next scene he's hanging someone."

It wasn't the first time someone had compared Jon's character to that of the fictional character he portrayed. It shook Maggie to realize that the Jonathan of her memories might be a figment of her imagination.

"He and my youngest son kept in touch, but I hadn't seen him in years. He was only ten when they moved."

Tanya frowned. "He talked about moving to L.A. It seemed to me that he resented the fact that they left Arizona. Even though it put him right there in the middle of things as far as his singing and acting."

Tanya rocked back and forth on her heels, her hands still in her pockets. Maggie wondered if she was feeling the cold the way her old bones were. Or was it nerves that kept the younger woman moving?

"Why did his family move, anyway? Did his father get transferred or something? Though now that I think about it, I never heard him mention his father."

"His father disappeared."

"Disappeared?" Tanya straightened and her hands came out of her pockets to rest at her side. "You mean he was, like, murdered or something?"

"No one knows exactly what happened to him. The assumption at the time was that he ran out on them. You've heard that old cliché about the man who says 'I'm going to the store for a pack of cigarettes' and then never comes back. At least that's what we all thought at the time. Carmen claims she moved because she was so embarrassed by it, though she did have family in L.A."

"Wow. Ran out on them. That must have been tough on a kid."

They were both silent for a moment. Maggie thought of the little boy she'd known and the adult he'd become. Apparently two very different people.

"So what really happened at the restaurant that night?"

Tanya sighed. "If I'd known the real Jonathan Hunter, I doubt I ever would have dated him. He dumped me that Sunday—right after the show."

"So, the reason you were too upset to go on that Tuesday, had nothing to do with losing the man you loved."

She nodded. "When I heard he'd been killed I was scared to death. The police questioned me with the others, of course. But they knew we'd been dating and one of the first things they asked was if we'd had any recent fights. I lied and told them we hadn't. I didn't think anyone knew about the disagreement we'd had. Though of course they all knew we weren't together at the dinner. The detective who questioned me seemed to imply that I was guilty, and it was just a matter of time until he could prove it. So by then, I was too upset to perform. And on Wednesday, I couldn't sing because of a cold. So it looked like I was really upset about Jon."

"What happened exactly that Sunday?"

"We all went out to dinner together. I guess you heard about that?"

Maggie nodded. "Did anything happen there?"

"Jon was feeling good, flirting outrageously. It had something to do with happy childhood memories and how he was going to recapture his youth."

"He'd looked at a piece of property—some land my family is selling, in fact. It's right near where he grew up."

"I was tired that day and getting a sore throat." Tanya's hand moved up to her neck as though protecting that important part of her anatomy. "I didn't want to go, but Jon did. He ended up making such a fuss, he told me not to ever expect to go out with him again. And, even though I knew he was a jerk by then, I hated that he was telling me off and so I tagged along. For all the good it did. He never even glanced at me. Sat right next to Susanne and hit on her instead. You should have seen the looks Roman was giving him."

"Susanne." Maggie suddenly glanced at her watch and groaned. "Oh, my. I have to see Susanne, too. Do you think she's already gone?"

Tanya gave her first real smile of the evening. "You might still catch her if you hurry. She's usually the last to leave. Takes her forever to take off her makeup."

Maggie called out her thanks as she fled down the path, hurrying as Tanya suggested. She was just in time. As she approached the door, she saw Susanne exit. Victoria stepped up to her and said something, effectively holding her while Maggie took the last few steps to reach them.

Maggie had to smile at Victoria's ingenuity. Why hadn't she thought of it herself? Victoria was handing Susanne a square of fabric to autograph, one of the blocks from the memory quilt.

"You're the last person from the cast that we need for the quilt," Victoria told her, as Susanne dutifully inscribed her name on the fabric.

As she handed over the signed block, Maggie took the bull by the horns. "You have Jonathan Hunter's car, don't you, Susanne?"

"What?" Her eyes flashed, but not with anger, Maggie suddenly realized. With fear. Her head moved from side to side as she scanned the parking lot. "I . . . I don't know what you're talking about."

"Come now." Maggie kept her voice quiet and gentle. There were still a few people moving about and Maggie didn't want to attract too much attention. About a hundred yards away, Jeff was just getting into his car, Judy and Kevin climbing in with him. Judy and Kevin waved to someone on the other side of the driveway, but Maggie couldn't see who it was. Jeff seemed to be staring right at her, his expression grim.

Maggie quickly turned back to Susanne. She would use Michael's technique—just accuse her of leaving with Jon and see what happened. It hadn't worked for Michael with Tanya, but Maggie thought that was because she really hadn't been with him later that night. Tanya's story about their quarrel certainly sounded genuine. "You left the restaurant that night with Jon. He drove you out to see the land he wanted to buy."

Maggie noted Susanne's "scared rabbit" expression and knew she'd have to do something quickly or the other woman would bolt. She took her arm and led them toward the pathway that would take them around the building. It was where she'd talked to Tanya and she knew it would be deserted there. "Maybe we can go somewhere to talk," she suggested, as she led her to the turn in the path that would keep them out of sight. "There's a coffee bar not too far from here."

But Susanne stopped and shook her head. "No. I don't want to go somewhere public." She turned toward Maggie and gripped her arm. Maggie almost winced from the strong grasp of her fingers. "We can go to my place. Or, rather, my cousin's place. He works the graveyard shift at the hospital, so we can have the place to ourselves. I'll . . ." She swallowed, her eyes focusing somewhere in the vicinity of Maggie's throat. As though she was ashamed to meet her eyes. "I'll tell you everything."

"Shall we take my car?" Maggie asked.

"Mine is right over here," Susanne said. "Why don't you let me drive and then I'll bring you back here to pick up your car."

Maggie and Victoria exchanged a meaningful look.

"We'll follow you," Victoria declared firmly.

Susanne burst into tears. "You think I'm a murderer."

Victoria wasn't going to deny something so obvious. But she could be diplomatic. "No, it means that I think it will be very late when we finish and we'll want to start straight for home. And there's no reason for you to come back here either; you'll be tired after your performance."

As they turned out of the parking lot behind Susanne's teal Escort, Maggie congratulated Victoria on her tactfulness.

Victoria acknowledged this with a nod. "She's a pretty little thing—it's hard to believe she might harm anyone. But why take chances?"

Chapter Twenty-three

Within minutes Susanne pulled into the driveway of a small house in a middle-class neighborhood of Tempe. The driveway wasn't deep enough for Maggie to pull in behind her, so she parked on the street.

"This is certainly convenient for you," Victoria commented, as they all met at the end of the driveway.

"That's why I'm staying here," Susanne replied. "And it works out well with Brent being on the graveyard shift. We both sleep days."

At the side of the garage, beside the big double door, was a normal-sized door with a glass insert. Susanne unlocked it, and stepped inside, flipping the light on. Parked there, shiny and new, was an Oldsmobile Bravada, metallic green paint, California plates spelling out PHNTM.

Maggie let out a long breath. "So you *were* the one with Jon that night."

A fresh bout of tears filled Susanne's eyes. "I thought you knew. . . ." She turned angry, accusing eyes toward Maggie.

"I mostly suspected. Tanya denied it and I believed her. And you were so frightened when I asked about the car."

Before their eyes, Susanne deflated. Her proud carriage became tired; her head drooped. And she sighed. "They had a fight at the theater. Tanya and Jon. Jon was feeling good. He was getting great reviews in the local press and he'd had a drink or two. He was telling everyone that he was taking his hometown by storm. That he was going to come back here a success. Buy land, build a house."

Susanne kept her eyes on the two women, as though reluctant to look at the car. She wiped the remnants of her tears from her face with the palms of both hands. "Would you like to come in and have some coffee? I usually have something to eat when I get home. I'll make decaf."

She opened the door beside them and they entered to find themselves in a cramped windowless laundry room. Another door led into a small, seventies-style kitchen. All the appliances were avocado green. While Susanne busied herself with the incongruously modern coffeemaker, Maggie excused herself. She hoped Susanne would think she was using the restroom. But instead she tiptoed through the house, easing the front door open, and stepped outside. She hurried back to the garage and stopped beside the truck. Suddenly, she realized that she couldn't just touch a vehicle that was an important part of a murder investigation. Reaching into her pocket, she found a linen handkerchief. She wrapped this around her hand and tried the driver's side door.

To Maggie's surprise, the door opened easily. The interior light illuminated the inside of the vehicle with its the lovely tan upholstery and carpet. The car retained that special "new car" aroma that was so enticing.

Maggie stood there, uncertain what else to do. She'd been drawn into this detecting game, however, and she knew she should look over the car while she had the chance. And she had to hurry, before the others missed her.

Quickly, Maggie tried to memorize the interior of the truck so that she could pull out the picture later and analyze it. There were no obvious clues like they always found on television shows—no matchbooks or unmatched earrings. There wasn't even any dirt or gravel, no dust or leaves or any of the other desert debris that usually littered the floor of Maggie's car. She wondered if Susanne had vacuumed the interior. Even if Jon had kept his car immaculate, its current condition seemed too pristine for a car that had been in use.

The seat seemed to be back as far as it would go. That was the only thing that struck Maggie as worth noting. Petite Susanne wouldn't have been able to drive it from that setting, but she might have pushed it back after it was parked. Especially if she'd vacuumed it.

With a sigh Maggie eased the door closed, pushing firmly on it until it closed with a muffled thump. Then she retraced her steps back to the kitchen.

"Goodness, Maggie, I thought you drowned in there," Victoria exclaimed when she finally reentered the kitchen.

Susanne, however, seemed oblivious to everything except her hostessing duties. She poured three cups of coffee and set them out on the table with sugar, sweetener, and milk. Then she brought out a bag of bagels and a carton of cream cheese. Finally she sat down and Maggie was able to steer her back to the last day of Jon's life.

"So you were telling us about leaving for the restaurant," Maggie reminded her.

Susanne seemed resigned to telling her tale, but certainly not eager. "Jon was flirting outrageously all night. With all the women, not just me." Susanne sliced a bagel in half and smeared it with cream cheese. But instead of taking a bite, she held it in her hand and examined it.

"This has been an emotional stopover for me. I haven't been getting on real well with my relatives. Some of them are jealous of my success." She broke off a bite-size piece of the bagel but continued to hold it between her fingers. "My older sister had wanted to go to New York or L.A. or even Vegas years ago. My parents talked her out of it. So now she's seeing me having some success and she can hardly stand it. She figures it should be her up there. But you know what? She was never good enough. She could never sing Christine."

Her lips drew together into a thin line, and finally, she put the bagel into her mouth. She chewed carefully while her eyes gleamed with pride in her own singing ability. That determination, Maggie thought, was what had made her defy her parents and pursue her career, and to achieve a certain amount of success. But had it led her somehow into murder? Maggie looked at the woman sitting beside her and could not bring herself to believe it. Was she too gullible? Or was Susanne innocent?

"So anyway, I was ready for a distracting flirtation." Susanne took a sip of her coffee, then pulled a pink packet from the bowl on the table and emptied the powder into her cup. She continued to speak as she stirred the mixture. "I don't think many people knew that Tanya and Jeff had a fight earlier that evening. But I'd heard them arguing about going out. Tanya said she wasn't feeling well and wanted to go straight home. Then she ended up coming anyway and Jon totally ignored her."

Susanne lowered her head, ashamed of her behavior that night. "Jon seemed to be picking me out, treating me real special. I was so flattered." She glanced up at the two older women, her eyes pleading. "He was so handsome. His voice was so wonderful."

Maggie nodded sympathetically.

"I guess Tanya finally had enough of his ignoring her. She attached herself to Jeff for dinner and when we finished I noticed they were whispering, their heads close together. Then they just disappeared. Jon seemed to get even more excited after that and I decided to go ahead and go with him. He was still talking about that land he was going to buy. He decided he had to see it again and he'd take me out to see it, too. I could hardly believe he wanted to take *me*."

Susanne dropped the spoon into the saucer with a loud clatter. "It's a relief to be telling this to someone. I haven't told a soul so far, not even my family. I can't sleep at night, can hardly eat. I keep waiting for the police to bang on the door and arrest me."

Maggie and Victoria exchanged a glance. Susanne did have dark circles under her eyes. The stage makeup covered it effectively, but now, with her face scrubbed clean after the performance, she looked more like a raccoon than a leading actress.

"We drove out to the property. It was late so there was no traffic. He drove out on this narrow road—no lights, of course. It was real dark. I felt like we were out in the middle of the desert, but he said we weren't. Then he finally stopped. I was beginning to get scared. You know, way out there in the middle of nowhere, with a guy I wasn't sure I trusted." Susanne picked up her bagel and broke off another piece. But she dropped it back onto her plate uneaten.

"I was beginning to think he'd made the whole thing up, just to get me alone out there. I hadn't seen any houses and I wondered if he had the right place. He got mad, said he knew where he was going. Then he said that this was the back way in, that he didn't want to disturb the neighbors so late at night."

"That was very considerate of him," Victoria said.

"Probably got him killed," Maggie murmured.

Susanne blinked, her lips trembled. But she managed to go on. "He got out of the car and started walking into the desert. He was talking about the stars and the air. . . . It was so dark. Then he told me to watch out for scorpions, can you imagine?" Her thin shoulders shivered with a delicate shudder. "I could hear his voice. I could tell he was moving away from me, but he was still talking about the land, how great it was, what he was going to do with it. He had grand ideas—a big house, swimming pool, tennis courts . . ."

She ran her tongue over her lips. Her hands clutched nervously together in front of her forgotten cup of sweetened coffee.

"Soon I couldn't hear him anymore. I called out, but he didn't answer. I thought he was playing some kind of game and I was getting mad. Scared, too. I didn't like being out there all alone, in the dark, in the desert. No houses around, the few lights I could see were pretty far away. And the little noises I heard were scaring me even more. I didn't know what might be out there. I wasn't born here, you know. My family moved here a few years ago; I never live here myself. I thought there might be coyotes and I've heard some stories about them out in L.A. And then Jon had gone and mentioned scorpions. He said they come out at night. I didn't know what else might be out there. And I didn't want to find out. I was getting real upset and screaming for Jon—"

She choked back a sob, lowering her voice at the same time. Maggie and Victoria strained to hear her. "My foot hit something. I almost lost my balance. And it was him." She swallowed hard. "Imagine if I had fallen over him—I would have landed on top of . . . of his body."

She shuddered again, violently this time. Maggie got up and brought over the coffeepot to top off her cup. She'd hardly drunk enough to allow for it, but Maggie added what she could, hoping the newly hot liquid would help. Susanne took a tentative sip, then another. It did seem to settle her somewhat. Finally she went on with her story.

"I couldn't believe it was Jon, then I thought he was playing some trick on me. But he didn't move and I finally realized he wasn't breathing. He was dead. And when I touched him, I got blood on my hand. And the thing of it was—there was no one there. Just me. And I thought, oh, no, they'll think I did it." Her voice rose. "There was no one else around. No one. Not even a coyote."

She took another sip of her coffee, wrapping her hands around the warm cup to help steady them. "I panicked. He'd left the keys in the car, so I just got in and drove off. I drove right on home and put his car in my cousin's garage. I told Brent I was putting up a friend's car while he was away. I told him it belonged to one of the cast members who had to fly to Chicago for a family emergency and he was afraid his car would get ripped off. I paid him fifty bucks for the use of the garage."

"It's been driving me crazy wondering what happened to that car," Maggie admitted.

"Well, now you know." Susanne pushed the coffee cup back and forth on its saucer, nudging the cup's handle with her index finger and thumb. "The police questioned all of us, of course. They questioned Tanya and me over and over again. And from the way they asked their questions I thought they must know I was there. But they kept asking who he left with that night. And no one said it was me. We had both driven over to the restaurant that night and we drove over to my place after dinner so I could leave my car. It was pretty late then, after one, I think."

"You poor thing. No wonder you can't sleep nights." Victoria was all sympathy.

"What am I going to do?"

"Let me think," Maggie said.

Victoria looked at Maggie, her eyes wide in surprise. "Why, she has to go to the police and tell them she was there."

"But we don't want her to get arrested," Maggie said. "Let me think," she repeated. "I wonder if I could ask Michael?"

"He'd have to report it," Victoria answered.

"You're right." Maggie nodded. "He'd have to, of course. My son is a police officer in Scottsdale," she told Tanya. "He's not working on this case, of course, but Victoria's right. It wouldn't be ethical for him to keep quiet about something like this."

Maggie was silent for a moment, thinking. "How can we prove someone else was out there? What about trace elements on the car?"

She looked over at Susanne who was shaking her head. "I was so scared, I took it to a car wash and had it cleaned inside and out."

Maggie frowned. "I was afraid of that. And then you drove it back here, so anything the police would find—fibers or whatever—would all be from you."

"Oh, no." Susanne was crying now, large tears running down her cheeks. "I didn't think of that."

"It would have been so much easier if you had just told the police all this that first day." Maggie sighed. "I'll let you know if I can think of any way out of this, but I can't see any now. You can't keep that car a secret forever and it would be better for you to call yourself. If you have a lawyer, he can call for you. What's the phone number here?"

Susanne took a paper napkin from an avocado-green plastic dispenser on the table, and wrote her phone number on it.

Maggie assured Susanne that she would call her the next day if any brilliant solution came to mind. "But I do think your best bet would be to get a lawyer and have him approach the police for you."

Susanne didn't appear happy with this recommendation. "Maybe you'll think of something else. You can call anytime. I haven't been sleeping much lately."

Maggie put her hand on the young woman's arm. "You'll probably rest better now that you've shared this all with someone else. I'm sure keeping it all inside wasn't good for you."

They parted at the small garage door, Maggie giving Susanne a reassuring hug before she headed down the drive. Victoria yawned mightily several times. When they were finally back in Maggie's car and heading home to Scottsdale, Victoria addressed her friend.

"Mary Margaret Browne. How could you advise that poor girl to stay home and be quiet? You know she has to tell the police. She should be calling them right now."

Maggie frowned. "Oh, Victoria, I don't know what to do right now. It's late, and I'm tired. But I'm sure that girl did not kill Jonathan. And I need a good night's sleep so that I can think more clearly about what she ought to do. I believe her story. I just wish I could think of who might have been out there that night."

Victoria recognized the stubborn tone that underlay her friend's words. There was no point to arguing with her now. She sighed. "Okay. But I hope you know what you're doing."

Maggie turned the car onto Scottsdale Road; her eyes feeling dry and scratchy after her long day. She hoped she knew what she was doing, too. "I'm sure I'm right about her. She's such a nice and sincere person."

"But do remember, Maggie. She's an actress. And a good one. She has the lead in this show."

Maggie sighed. "I should have known none of this would be easy."

"I agree she did sound sincere. Maybe that's why I wondered." Victoria looked thoughtful. "What if he was playing games with her—as she had suspected? It could have frightened her badly. She said her mind was churning with thoughts of what might be out there. From what we've heard, Jon wasn't quite the sweet, polite young man you remember. He could be mischievous and even mean."

Maggie had to agree. "I'm afraid you're right. Maybe I only want to remember the good things about his childhood days." She sighed, remembering the child singing in the kitchen. She liked the child much better than the man she was hearing about.

"So, what if she's calling for him, getting panicky," Victoria continued. "And he's playing around, hiding from her. Then maybe jumps out at her. He could be crouching down, which would put his head down at her level. She's so frightened she lashes out at him—and all of a sudden, he's lying there with a gash in his head, and she doesn't know what to do."

"I have to admit that sounds about as likely as anything else," Maggie agreed.

"I just want you to be careful around her," Victoria cautioned.

Maggie stopped at a red light, frustrated by both the lack of cross traffic and by the progress—or lack thereof—in the investigation into Jon's death. "Will we ever get to the end of this?"

Chapter Twenty-four

It was a lovely morning: sunny blue skies, temperatures in the seventies, birds singing in the courtyard trees. The sound of water falling in the nearby fountain should have ensured a scene of peace and tranquility. But the women seated around the quilt frame beneath the olive tree were agitated. Maggie had just finished a lengthy retelling of her meetings with Tanya and Susanne the previous night.

"Do you think she called the police?" Louise asked.

"I called her this morning and told her I couldn't see any way out of it. I suggested again that she call a lawyer and give herself up. She's a witness if nothing else."

"And she does have that car," Victoria reminded her.

"Oh, no." Maggie looked up to see Carmen coming in the gate. "Better not mention any of this to Carmen," she warned the others as her former neighbor walked across the courtyard toward them. "I don't know what she might do if we tell her I saw Jon's car last night."

The other Bee members murmured quick agreements, called out greetings to Carmen, but continued to work. The fan quilt was almost done and they were anxious to keep working on it.

As usual when she came to visit with them, Carmen sat at one corner of the frame. This time, however, Maggie invited her to sew a few stitches into the quilt. "You've been practicing during your last visits and your stitches are very nice. Your sewing experience shows."

Carmen glowed at the praise. "Well, if you're sure. I'd be proud to sew on your quilt."

"So, tell us more about that tall, good-looking man who was at the funeral," Anna urged.

Carmen, concentrating on putting in her first stitches, kept her head down. But Maggie could still see the blush that stained her cheeks. As she pulled the needle through, Carmen looked up. "Oh, Harley is an old friend. He was our neighbor, years ago, and he was a big help after Ed disappeared."

Once again Maggie was struck by the way Carmen always referred to Ed's defection as a disappearance. Why didn't she just say he took off? Then she scolded herself for being insensitive. Carmen had been embarrassed enough to move out of the state, where no one knew what had happened. She more than likely couldn't bring herself to use the blunt words, so chose the more discreet "disappearance."

"They haven't arrested anybody yet in your son's death." Edie just dropped her comment into the brief silence. Anna gasped and Victoria raised her eyebrows.

"No." Carmen sniffed delicately. "I've tried to talk to the detective in charge of the case, but he won't tell me anything."

"Probably doesn't know anything," was Edie's opinion. "And doesn't want to admit it. We probably know more than they do."

Heads around the frame all snapped up. Maggie glared at Edie, who had the grace to look embarrassed. She pulled her lips into a straight line and turned her eyes back to her stitching.

"We like to compare what we've heard to books we've read," Clare explained. "My first theory was that the understudy killed him so that he could have the role for himself."

Carmen had stopped sewing and just stared at Clare. "You think Jeff Manchester killed my Jon?"

Clare shrugged. "I read a book like that once." She finished off a thread and clipped another, but held it in her hand for a moment, the needle still stuck into the quilt top where she'd left it. "But then I met Jeff and Kevin, and they were both so nice. I did think there was something Jeff was trying to hide, though." She finished threading her needle and checked the quilt, looking for a place to start her new thread. "Actually, I just finished a book that gave me another good idea."

"What is it?" The question came simultaneously from both Louise and Anna. Maggie and Edie looked skeptical. They wanted to hear this new idea first.

"It was a great mystery. It had to do with a supposed suicide. But to solve the current mystery, the detective—an amateur," she added with significant emphasis, "has to go back twenty years to something that happened when she was a girl. It was a great story."

"And your point is?" Maggie asked.

"Maybe the answer to Jon's death is in the past."

"In the past?" Louise repeated.

"But you said your detective went back to her childhood. What would we go back to?" Victoria asked.

"To Jon's childhood, I guess," Clare replied. "Maybe to the time in Scottsdale, just before you moved, Carmen."

Maggie joined the others in looking over to Carmen. To Maggie's surprise, the color was gone from Carmen's face. The pink blush she'd applied to her cheeks showed up in stark contrast to the color of her skin, and the red on her lips suddenly appeared garish.

"It was such a long time ago," Carmen mumbled. Her fingers suddenly turned jerky and she pulled the needle she'd just inserted from the quilt. Leaving it loose on top of the fabric, she rose from her chair. "Excuse me. My stomach . . . it must be something I ate—" She rushed off toward the women's restroom, her hands held to her midsection.

Victoria started to rise, ready to follow and offer her help, but Maggie stopped her. "No, Victoria. I don't think you should follow her. She needs some time alone."

"But she might be ill."

Maggie shook her head and Louise, a former nurse, agreed. "It's something else. She turned pale when you mentioned checking into the past."

Maggie nodded. "Makes you wonder, doesn't it?"

Clare, instantly contrite, pulled her newly threaded needle through the fabric layers. She popped the knot through with a practiced motion. "Oh, dear. I didn't mean to upset her. Do you think something happened between Jon and someone else that made them leave? But that was so long ago—he was only a boy."

Maggie looked thoughtful. "I don't think it's that. You're right about him being young. The boys were only ten when they left. I doubt if a quarrel at that age could trigger a revenge killing twenty years later."

"Didn't you tell us they left after Carmen's husband disappeared?" Victoria asked. "Maybe that time is just too painful for her to remember. He never did come back, did he?"

"No. He just disappeared. Michael told me once that Jon tried to trace him, and the detective they hired didn't turn up anything."

"Oh, it's just like a mystery novel," Anna declared.

Clare agreed. "I think I read one like this, too."

The others groaned. Clare had a book to illustrate every situation. Maggie wished her memory was half as good.

"The wife and her boyfriend killed her husband and buried the body," Clare explained. "The police thought the husband had just run off, but years later when the house sold, the new owners dug in the backyard for a new fence . . ." Her voice grew lower as she enjoyed the telling of the story. "And they found a skeleton."

"Did they arrest the wife?" Anna asked.

"Oh, yes. And the boyfriend. And then the daughter remembered actually seeing the murder and the burial. The story was mainly about her, you see. Kind of a psychological story about all the trauma she went through over the years until it was all brought out in the trial. All her life she'd had bad dreams and then it turned out they weren't dreams at all. They were childhood memories."

"Interesting story," Louise admitted. "But that was just a story, Clare. In real life things are pretty different."

"I'll say." Edie huffed. "In real life they would never have solved it. The wife would get away with it. The husband was probably a real bum, too—probably deserved it."

"He might have been a—" Anna's voice dropped so the others strained to hear. It was as though she hated to say the word aloud, ashamed to admit there might be people of that type who actually existed. "—a wife abuser," she finished.

"Here comes Carmen," Victoria warned. Her voice rose as she called across to her. "Are you feeling better?"

Carmen returned to her chair but did not pick up her needle. "A little."

Maggie thought her color did appear better. She'd probably splashed some water on her face, removing some of the makeup. Without the contrast to the artificial color, she still looked pale, just not so ill.

"How about some tea?" Anna asked, rising before Carmen had a chance to agree. "Some nice herbal tea would be just the thing."

As Anna headed for the kitchen where coffee and tea were always available, Victoria turned to Carmen. "Why don't you and Maggie tell us about Jon and Michael as boys. I never had any children of my own, but I taught for many years. I do enjoy stories about children and their antics."

Carmen smiled and Maggie had to admire Victoria's technique. Carmen seemed more than willing to talk about Jon's childhood. So why had she reacted so strongly to a suggestion that the answer to the identity of Jon's killer lay in the past?

After the Quilting Bee, Maggie and Victoria headed over to Maggie's. They planned to have lunch and then sew together the memory quilt blocks. Over chicken salad and cantaloupe slices, Victoria and Maggie rehashed the morning's discussions.

"Did you hear Edie's latest?" Victoria asked. "She implied that Carmen and Harley were picking up an intimate relationship from all those years ago. She thought that's why Carmen got so upset when Clare mentioned the past. She said they probably killed her husband and hid the body. I told Edie she's been watching too many soap operas."

But Maggie wasn't laughing. "I hate to admit agreeing with Edie on something like this, but I've been wondering the same thing." She chewed thoughtfully for a moment. "We were all fairly certain that Ed was abusive. Not that Carmen ever said a word. But it was a sparsely populated area, so those of us who lived out there were close. Sometimes when we had a neighborhood get-together, Ed would have a bit to drink. And he could get nasty. Try to pick fights. He wasn't a big man and like most bullies, he wasn't brave. So nothing ever came of it with the other men. But Carmen's a little thing, so he could have bullied her easily."

"And with Jon there to see." Victoria's voice was sad.

"I even found myself wondering the other day if maybe Jon killed his dad. To save his mother. I wonder if I got the idea from a movie-of-the-week ad. But then I realized how silly that idea was, given Jon's age at the time."

Maggie broke off a piece of the dill bread Victoria had contributed to their lunch. She held it in her hand, untasted, while her mind continued to work on the problem. "But Carmen and Harley . . . Now that's a workable idea." She put the bread in her mouth, savoring the light, delicious flavor. "Harley's place is right near where Carmen used to live. She and Ed had a little tiny place. He mostly hired out to other ranchers in the area. And she had a large vegetable garden."

"A vegetable garden, huh?"

Maggie and Victoria's eyes met across the table, both of them remembering Clare's comments about bodies buried in backyards. They began to laugh. Movie of the week indeed!

Chapter Twenty-five

By the time they finished lunch, Maggie realized she had to pay a visit to some of her old neighbors. She apologized to Victoria. "I know I asked you to come over and help sew together the quilt for Carmen, but with everything that's been said today about the past—I don't know. I think I'd like to go over and reminisce with some of my old neighbors. See what might come up."

"Don't you worry about me." Victoria put the last dish in the dishwasher and straightened up. "If you give me the blocks, I can sew them together this afternoon and return them to you before we head to Tempe this evening."

Maggie threw Victoria a wide grin. "I was hoping you'd say that." She gave her a hug. "What would I do without you?"

Maggie drove through her old neighborhood with mixed emotions. Although she visited the area often, today she seemed to see it through new eyes. It was definitely not the same place she had come to as a starry-eyed bride. There had been so many changes over the years. Developers had discovered the beauty of the area near the mountains, and the many small ranches were now numerous suburban subdivisions, filled with beige stuccoed houses bearing the ever-present red-tiled roofs. But in the older ranch-style homes sprinkled among the subdivisions, some of the same people she'd known still resided.

Maggie enjoyed her afternoon visiting her old neighbors. She began with Winona Winthrop, sitting through a recitation of dear Samson's troubles, awaiting her chance to reminisce about the old days.

"Remember how we'd all get together for a barbecue on Labor Day?" Maggie was finally able to ask.

"Oh, yes." Winona's smile was bright. "Those were good times, weren't they? All your little boys. Such lovely children."

"Jon Hunter, too. He was always over at my place. Such a beautiful little boy."

Winona nodded pleasantly. "Yes, he was." Samson lay beside her on the couch and she rubbed his ears absently. "Those barbecues were fun, weren't they? It's just not the same these days. The new people who come in hardly stop to say hello. They're all so busy. I barely know the neighbor to the east. They have lived there a whole year, but I never see them. I went over when they moved in, introduced myself. They were friendly enough, but that was it. Never saw them again. Not like the old days, when we'd all get together to welcome newcomers. Remember when Harley married and brought his wife home? We had a morning coffee for her. I made my cinnamon-raisin coffee cake."

Maggie remembered those days fondly herself. And Winona had provided just the opening she needed. "I was trying to remember if we'd had a get-together for Carmen. It's been nice seeing her again, don't you think?"

Winona hardly seemed to hear Maggie's final question. At mention of a get-together, her lips pulled a straight line and she fairly glowered. "We'd planned one for Carmen. I still remember it. That husband of hers wouldn't let her come. Called at the last minute and made some ridiculous excuse." Winona leaned forward to offer Maggie more tea. When Maggie refused, she added more to her own cup. "That man was no darn good. Don't know why she ever married him, a pretty girl like her."

"Yes, I remember now. I don't see how I could have forgotten. For a while, Ed didn't even want Jon to play at our place. But then he must have realized how odd that appeared to everyone and he let Jon come over whenever he wanted."

Winona smiled. "That boy used to live over at your place."

"He was very sweet, though. And never any bother."

"Probably afraid to create any conflict."

Maggie stared at Winona.

Winona shrugged. "You know we all talked about it at the time. Ed was a thoroughly disagreeable man. We all of us said he probably hit them." She ended with a definitive nod. "Jon was such a slight child while Ed was strong and muscular. And Jon was as afraid of him as Carmen was. Wouldn't have surprised me to hear she'd killed him, when he disappeared. But the body was never found and I don't think she could have hidden it that well."

"Don't you think he just ran away? I remember thinking that he was just the type to go out for cigarettes and never come back. I always wondered if he'd found some woman willing to support him and run off with her."

"That would've been like him," Winona agreed. "But I think he must've died sometime soon after. No one's ever been able to track him down."

Maggie nodded. "Yes, I heard the same thing. I guess Carmen and Jon tried too."

"Don't know why they'd bother. If it was me, I'd have said good riddance and forgotten about him."

Yes, Maggie thought. That's what she would have done, too.

Further visits turned up similar opinions. All her old friends remembered the old days fondly. All lamented the loss of neighborliness. Everyone urged Maggie to visit more often. And universally, everyone disliked Ed Hunter.

It was a wonder the police didn't look into it as a murder case, Maggie thought. He was so universally disliked, why didn't they think someone killed him?

Finally, Maggie drove to Hal's. She went down the driveway past the house and pulled in beside the barn. A ride on Chestnut would be just the thing before she headed home. As she neared the barn, she waved over at Sara, weeding a flower bed along the back of the house. She should go over and say hello, but she was all visited out. She knew Sara would understand.

Maggie stopped as she stepped into the dim interior of the barn. Her old eyes needed a moment to readjust from the bright sun outside.

"Why, howdy, Miz Browne."

As Maggie's eyes became accustomed to the dim interior, she spotted Jimmy laying hay in a stall. Her wide smile was genuine. It was always a pleasure to see old Jimmy. A grizzled and picturesque cowboy, he'd worked for them since the early days. He was well over eighty now, but he still liked to help Hal out.

"Jimmy. It's always a pleasure to see you."

Jimmy ducked his head in embarrassment. He mumbled something which might have been "nice to see you, too," but Maggie couldn't be sure. He knew why she had come and was already leading Chestnut out.

"I've had a pleasant afternoon, Jimmy, visiting with some of the old neighbors. I'm surprised at how many of the old-timers still live out this way."

Not much of a talker, Jimmy just nodded; he was already lifting the saddle over Chestnut's back.

"We talked a lot about the old days, back when we used to have neighborhood get-togethers and barbecues. Remember that?"

Jimmy nodded once again. A fast worker even at his age, he had Chestnut all ready for her ride.

Maggie smiled at Jimmy fondly. "You and Harry did a lot of barbecuing in those days." She approached Chestnut and ran her hand along the animal's neck. The horse nuzzled her hip, checking for treats that might be hidden in her pockets. "Do you remember Ed Hunter?"

"No-good no-account."

Well, that was succinct, Maggie thought. "That does seem to be the general opinion," she stated. "I wonder whatever happened to him."

"Probably killed himself," was Jimmy's opinion.

"What makes you say that?" Maggie knew you had to ask specific questions to get anything out of the taciturn Jimmy.

"Saw him that last night. He was heading for the mountain with a bottle in his hand. He was a drinker, that Ed. And mean with it. Probably drank the whole bottle and tumbled off a ledge."

"But wouldn't someone have found his body?"

"You go far enough into the mountains back there, Miz Browne, and no one'll ever find you."

With that warning ringing in her ears, Maggie left for her ride. She kept to the Browne property, suddenly worried about becoming lost. Could that be the answer to the riddle of Ed Hunter? Had he stumbled around the desert in the dark—drunk—and fallen somewhere? Then died of exposure? Twenty years later, they probably would never know.

Chapter Twenty-six

Victoria arrived early at Maggie's doorstep that evening. The memory quilt was neatly folded over her arm. "I've decided to drive tonight. You've been busy 'detecting' all day and you can use the time to relax. And you can tell me everything you learned while I drive."

They took a moment long enough to unfold the quilt and admire it; then the two women got into Victoria's Buick and headed south. Maggie spent the drive time recounting her visits with her old friends.

"Well, that certainly is interesting," Victoria commented. "I agree with you. Nobody seemed to like that man and then he just disappeared. It does seem like it would have borne some looking into."

"Well, I'm sure the police did look into it at the time. But I can't help thinking they dismissed it as a runaway husband when there might have been more to it."

Victoria agreed as they pulled into the Gammage lot. "I had a student whose father disappeared. The police looked into it briefly, decided he'd just run off on his responsibilities. But the family refused to consider it and they got their friends to help them search. It took almost a year, but they found his body in the desert. He'd been murdered. They never found the killer, of course. Too much time had passed."

Victoria and Maggie stepped out of the car, moving behind it into the driving lane of the parking lot. The sudden sound of a car engine revving made them turn their heads.

A small white car was speeding down the path, moving much too fast for a parking lot. Startled, the two women stood stock still for two seconds that felt like sixty. Then Maggie came to, adrenaline pumping through her. Pushing Victoria back toward the car, she jumped to the side, toward the support pillars of Frank Lloyd Wright's long walkways that led down from the balconies. Maggie swore she felt the car brush her skirt, but neither woman was injured. Two other volunteers, also just exiting their vehicles, came rushing over.

"Are you all right?"

Shaky but refusing to be intimidated, Maggie brushed herself off and checked on the condition of her friend. "I'm fine. Victoria, are you okay?"

"Yes. Oh, Maggie. Someone's trying to kill you!"

The other volunteers stared at her. Maggie wondered if they thought the shock of the incident had gotten to Victoria. But they led Maggie and Victoria inside and reported what they had seen.

Duane, the house manager, was instantly solicitous and called the ASU police. They sent someone over to take a report, but there wasn't too much they could do. None of the six or so people who saw the incident could do more than say it was a small white car. Makes and models varied from one person to the next. No one had glimpsed the license plate. They all thought it was a local plate but couldn't really say. No one saw the driver, though more than one of the older people decided it had to be a young person.

"They're always in such a dog-goned hurry to get somewheres," Eugene declared.

Although Maggie tried to put on a brave face, she was badly shaken. She and Victoria sat together, comforting each other. Maggie was actually shaken enough to call Michael, who rushed over. He told the officers about the threat Maggie had received previously, a detail that had completely fled her mind.

Now he stood before her, scowling. But Maggie knew it was fear for her safety that caused the fierce look.

"Are you all right, Ma?"

"Yes. We weren't hurt. There were quite a few other people around."

Michael ran a hand through his already disheveled hair. "Come on, I'll take you two home."

"But we can't leave Victoria's car here."

"Do you really think you should drive after what happened?"

Maggie gave her youngest son her best stern look. "I would not have wanted to drive right after it happened, but that was," she glanced at her watch, "over an hour ago. If Victoria can't drive her car home, I'll do it for her. We'll be fine, won't we, Victoria?"

Her friend was still very pale, but she nodded bravely. "I think my legs are steady enough now to take me to the car and my heartbeat is almost normal. But I think I'll let you drive," she added with a smile toward Maggie.

Michael frowned at the two women. But he noted the gleam in his mother's eye. No use arguing with her once she got that look. "Okay. But I'll follow you home. No argument."

Back at Victoria's condo, Maggie, Victoria, and Michael congregated in the kitchen. *Funny how we always gravitate toward the kitchen when we need comfort,* Maggie thought. Victoria bustled about making coffee and setting out some homemade shortbread. But no one was eating.

Michael pulled out a chair at the table but didn't sit down. Instead, he paced back and forth in the cramped kitchen, his athletic shoes making little squeaking noises on the tile floor. With a grimace at the irritating little squeals, he finally sat and picked up his coffee cup. The hot liquid did nothing to ease the tightness that clutched his chest.

"Ma, I told you not to get involved. You're gone too far this time."

Maggie didn't know what to say. She knew he was frightened for her. "I really don't know what I've done, Michael."

"This is serious, Ma."

"I know. And I'm serious, too. I visited some old neighbors today. That's all."

Victoria cleared her throat. Both Michael and Maggie looked over. In their concern for each other they'd forgotten she was in the room.

"What about Susanne?"

Michael looked from Victoria to his mother in bewilderment. "Susanne? You mean the woman in the play? What does she have to do with this?"

Maggie sighed in resignation and told Michael about her activities the previous night.

" 'All I did today was visit some old friends,' " he parodied when she'd finished. "For goodness sakes, Ma, didn't it occur to you that what you've been doing the last few days might carry over?" He ran his fingers through his hair in frustration. "Why didn't you at least come to me with this? What if she's the murderer?"

"Well . . ." Maggie regretted waiting now, but she'd felt deeply that it was up to Susanne to turn herself in. She was disappointed in the girl. "You would have had to report it to your superiors, you see, and I was so sure she didn't kill him."

"Come on, Ma. How can you be sure?"

"Well, I believe she's a sincere young woman, who got caught up in all this through no fault of her own."

Michael raised a speculative brow. "No fault of her own? She went off with him in the middle of the night, to the middle of nowhere, didn't she?"

Maggie sighed. There were no easy answers. "I really thought she would call the police today and tell them all about it herself. She practically promised me."

Michael shook his head. "You're too gullible, Ma. That's why you have to leave these things to the professionals."

"There's one thing that's been bothering me," Maggie told him. "Just how was Jon killed?"

Michael paused, his cup raised halfway to his lips. "Ma."

Maggie heard the warning in his voice but chose to ignore it. "Humor me. What can it hurt? Besides, the paper reported that he died from a heavy blow to the head. I just wanted you to verify that that was correct."

It was Michael's turn to sigh. "It is. A large rock has been identified as the murder weapon. A weapon of opportunity."

"Or passion."

"You see what I'm trying to tell you?"

"No, Michael, I don't. You're letting your concern for me interfere with your rational police officer's mind. Now, just think about it for a second. Have you seen Susanne?"

Michael shook his head. "No. She didn't appear the night we saw the show, did she? And she wasn't at the barbecue."

Maggie looked smug. "Well, I've talked to her face to face. She's about five-foot-two, nice figure but very thin. I doubt she weighs more than a hundred pounds. One-ten at the very most." However, since she liked Susanne, she didn't mention the strength she'd felt in that delicate hand when Susanne grasped her arm the night before. She also refrained from telling him about Victoria's speculation on the position Jon may have been in when he was hit.

Michael stared at her, a frown creasing the laugh lines around his mouth. "Okay. I see your point."

"How big a rock?"

"Oh, about—" Michael stopped himself, his lips tipping into a smile. "Oh, no, you don't."

He actually shook his finger at her, as if she was a naughty child!

"Besides, size isn't everything," he added, and Maggie knew she wasn't hiding anything by keeping Victoria's theory to herself. “He could have been sitting or stooping. Or she could have climbed on something.”

“I just wanted to get an idea of the size. Jon wasn’t a really big man after all. He looked large on stage because he dominated the show, but he wasn’t quite six feet tall and slight of build. You remember how the other boys teased him when he was young because he was so delicately built.”

Michael nodded. Jon had often been the target of bullies because of his size and the fact that he liked to sing and perform. Michael had tried to get him involved in riding and other “manly” pursuits but he’d had limited success.

“A lot of the actors are small people. Remember I’ve met all of them now and I’ve been surprised at how different they look in person. Judy looks so tall and regal as Carlotta, but offstage she’s my height and very humble.”

“That’s a good point,” Michael conceded. “And I’m sure the police have taken it into consideration. But I’ll be sure to mention it to Detective Warner when I talk to him.” He glanced at his watch. “Which I should do right now. “I’m sure he’ll want to talk to Susanne after the show.” He stood and took a few steps toward the wall phone before stopping. He turned back to his mother. “What’s the address where she has the car?”

Maggie shook her head. “I don’t know. We followed her there.”

Michael frowned and looked to Victoria but she shook her head as well. “Maggie got the phone number though.”

“Goodness, I almost forgot.” Maggie reached for her purse and soon had the rumpled paper napkin with the scribbled phone number on it. Almost reluctantly, she handed it to her son.

“Good.” Michael accepted the napkin from his mother, took the cordless phone from the wall and retreated to the living room. Maggie and Victoria could hear the drone of his voice as he reported to the detective.

"I just cannot bring myself to believe that that young woman killed Jonathan," Maggie declared.

"I know," Victoria agreed. "But still, someone had to do it. And she has his car."

Maggie nodded sadly. "Circumstantial. But incriminating just the same."

It was quite some time before Michael returned to the kitchen. He replaced the phone on the wall charger and refreshed his coffee before facing the two women. He took a long sip. "Well, I've reported everything to Detective Warner. He hasn't heard a thing from your sincere little actress but he'll be waiting to see her this evening. He'll want to talk to you too. Both of you."

He finished his coffee in a few quick gulps and checked his watch. "Come on, Ma, I'll walk you home. You can both expect visits from the police this evening. And make sure you tell them everything you know. Got that? Everything," he emphasized.

Victoria and Maggie both stood up. Maggie rolled her eyes at Victoria as she pulled on her sweater. She felt childish doing it, but she was sure Michael couldn't see her, and it made her feel better. "I've told you everything now." Maggie looked to her friend for corroboration. "Haven't I, Victoria?"

Victoria conceded that she had.

"Good. Maybe I should spend the night in your guest room, just to keep an eye on you."

Maggie winced. "Honestly, Michael. Just because there was a reckless driver in the parking lot this evening doesn't mean someone is trying to kill me."

"But we can't be sure they're not, either." His voice was firm. "Something strange is going on here and I'll feel a whole lot better when Susanne is in jail."

Chapter Twenty-seven

For once, the needles of the Quilting Bee women stilled and slowed as they talked across the frame that Thursday morning. Working at the very center of the fan quilt now, they expected to finish by the end of the day's session. If they could concentrate enough to actually work. Louise, Clare, Anna, and Edie could hardly believe the story Maggie and Victoria told of the previous night's escapade. Then Carmen joined them halfway through the account and Maggie had to start all over again.

"I'm sure I would have fainted dead away," Anna said when she'd finished.

"And been run over for sure as you lay there," Edie remarked.

Louise reassured Anna. "Your body responds better than you might expect when faced with situations like that. The adrenaline kicks in and helps out. Survival is one of the most primal of instincts."

Carmen had gasped when Maggie reported that the car actually brushed her skirt as it went by her. "I think you'd better be careful, Maggie. I know I asked for your help early on, but it's becoming dangerous. I wish you'd leave it alone now."

Anna nodded in agreement.

"Do you think the police will be able to catch the person who tried to run you down?" Clare asked.

"Doesn't seem likely," Edie intoned.

For once, Maggie was forced to agree with Edie. "None of us saw the plate number. Or even got a good look at the car. And it might just have been an accident."

Anna was relieved to hear Maggie say it might have been an accident after all. "So you don't think someone was deliberately trying to hit you? Or scare you off?"

"I think it's a possibility," Maggie declared. Victoria looked less certain.

"What was it like being interviewed by the police?" Clare asked.

Carmen winced. "You really don't want to know," she murmured.

"It's quite intimidating," Victoria told them.

"I agree," Maggie said. "I can understand now why you were so upset afterward, Carmen. Detective Warner asked all kinds of tough questions. And he was not at all happy at what he called my 'interference' in his murder investigation."

Victoria and Maggie were still answering questions about their interviews the previous evening when Rosalie from the church office approached the women under the olive tree. The sound of her heels clicked across the courtyard tiles like the staccato bursts of a carpenter's hammer. "Oh, Maggie," she called. "You have a very important call in the office." Her eyes widened slightly and her voice took on a whisper of intrigue as she imparted her news. "It's a police officer."

Maggie got up, but she waved her hand carelessly at the others. "It might just be Michael," she reminded them.

"I hope so," Carmen murmured.

Maggie wasn't gone long. "New developments." Her voice was sharp and brisk as she looked at Victoria. "The ASU police want to speak to us sometime today, Victoria. I told them we'd go down after lunch."

"Do you think you should wait?" Anna asked.

"Did they arrest someone about the incident last night?" Disheartened over the news she'd received, Maggie could still appreciate Victoria's sensitive wording. It reminded her of Carmen's delicate references to her husband's "disappearance."

Looking at the expectant faces around the quilt frame, she knew that the others wanted to hear the news. But thinking of the young man involved made her heartsick. She'd seen the show so many times now, spoken to most of the actors more than once. They were all beginning to feel like friends. And they were all so young. "They think it might be Roman Maggiore who tried to run us down last night." The tone of her voice told it all—sadness, regret.

"That young man who dances so beautifully?" Victoria asked.

"But why would he want to harm you?" Anna inquired.

"He must be involved in killing Jon," Louise said matter-of-factly. "Otherwise it makes no sense. Remember Maggie had that note telling her to back off."

"A note?" Carmen's voice rose. "You mean you've been threatened before?"

Maggie had to smile at Louise's rephrasing of the note she'd received. And she hastened to reassure Carmen. "Oh, it was nothing."

"But why would Roman want to harm Jon?" Much as Carmen wanted the killer of her son found, she couldn't understand why the young dancer would want to kill him. "It doesn't make any sense that he would have been involved." Her voice hardened. "Now if it had been Tanya or Susanne . . ."

"Or Jeff . . ." Clare contributed.

Maggie barely heard her. She was staring at Carmen. Why was she so set on the women? Was it jealousy? "The police were going to question Susanne last night. But I don't think there's enough evidence for them to arrest her."

"Didn't they question her right afterward? They even questioned me, like I had reason to kill my son." Carmen was still indignant about what she considered accusations by the detective in charge.

"Well, there was some new evidence," Victoria told her. "So they had to question her again."

Maggie sighed. Now that the police had the car, there was no point in trying to keep it from Carmen. "Susanne had Jon's car."

"What?" Carmen abandoned her needle. She was done with sewing for the day.

"Tanya told me that she and Jon had a disagreement that Sunday after the show, and he started flirting with Susanne. Susanne said Jon invited her to go for a drive with him after that dinner they all had together . . . to show her the land he wanted to buy. But when they got out there, it was so dark, he walked far ahead of her and she fell way behind, lost. She kept on walking and then tripped over his body."

Carmen's features hardened as she listened to the tale. "Who does she think she's kidding? Was there someone else out there with them?"

Maggie shook her head. "That's why she's so frightened. She felt sure she would be blamed. So she drove the car back to Tempe and parked it in her cousin's garage."

Carmen still didn't believe it. Maggie could tell by the look on her face.

"The only evidence they have against her is that car." Maggie tried to make her see what she did—there *was* no evidence.

"Sounds like plenty of evidence to me," Edie decided.

"But what does all this have to do with Roman?" Anna wanted to know.

Maggie shrugged. "I know they're very good friends. Maybe more. I've seen them together several times and he's very protective of her. Maybe he was trying to scare us away." Maggie finally sat back down and picked up her needle. "I don't know why they want us to come down. Maybe to look at his car? I told them I couldn't possibly identify the driver. I'm not even sure I could identify the car. It all happened too fast."

Victoria agreed. "I feel the same way."

Louise took them back to the night of the barbecue. "So which one was Roman?" she asked. "Such an unusual name, but I'm not sure I recall him."

"You'd remember if you saw him," Victoria said. "Roman is the one with the classic Italian good looks. Long, dark hair worn in a ponytail. He's in the first scene of the play—the one that's supposed to be an opera. He's the slave master leading the dancing girls."

"Good-looking young men, near-miss car accidents . . ." Clare's voice was filled with hard-to-suppress excitement. "Oh, it's just like a mystery novel."

Louise gave her a sharp look. "No, it's not, Clare. This isn't a novel, it's real. And Maggie almost died last night because she's been asking questions. The investigators in novels don't die."

Clare was instantly contrite. "The amateur detective never dies," she agreed. "But sometimes they do get hurt."

The comment sobered them all, Maggie included. Even though she felt Louise was exaggerating outrageously, a sudden chill ran through her, causing her hand to tremble. She pinned her needle into the quilt top and pushed back her chair. "I think I'm ready for a cup of tea."

"I'll go with you," Louise said, pressing her needle into the top.

As they headed for the kitchen, Louise put her arm around Maggie's shoulders. "Are you all right? Really?"

Maggie nodded. "I'm fine. Really."

Louise gave her shoulders a squeeze and released her. "That's good. But don't try to be too brave. I know you come from good pioneer stock and can face just about anything. But sometimes you have to admit to needing some help. And the shock of something like a murder attempt can linger, causing problems long after the event."

Louise was an R.N. and knew what she was saying. But Maggie didn't feel the need to unburden on her friend's shoulders. "Thank you for caring, Louise. But, really, everything is fine. And if it suddenly hits me in a week or two, I'll give you a call."

With that, they poured their tea and sat for a while with some of the seniors from the other craft groups. The break was just what Maggie needed. These people didn't know about the person who tried to run her down last night; they wouldn't bombard her with questions she couldn't answer.

Could it really be that attractive young man who'd tried to run them down? Maggie thought Roman had that tragic look some young dramatists intentionally create—for atmosphere. He reminded her of the young poets in their dark turtlenecks back in the days of the Beat Generation. He had that same lost look, the same resentment of authority. Perhaps he had . . .

Maggie was brought back to the present by a repeated mention of her name. "I'm sorry. Woolgathering, I'm afraid. What did you say?"

"We heard you knew that young man who was murdered? The actor, Jon Hunter? What was he like?"

"Well, he was just a boy when I knew him. . . ."

When Maggie and Louise returned from their break, Edie and Victoria were putting the last stitches in the fan quilt. Carmen was gone.

"She's meeting Harley for lunch," Clare reported. "Again." She and Anna were gathering up the basting pins, needles, scissors, and spools of thread and putting them away in their boxes. They were ready to unpin the quilt from the frame when Michael appeared at the gate. Maggie thought he looked very handsome in his tan uniform. But she had less than a minute to admire him before her mother's genes kicked in and she became worried.

"Michael. What are you doing here? Is everything all right? Hal and the boys . . . ?" She took a step toward him.

"Everything's fine. I was in the area and thought I'd see how you were doing." Michael walked up to her and planted a kiss on her cheek.

"Tell him about the call," Anna said.

Michael looked down at her, brows raised in question.

"I had a call from the ASU police. They think Roman Maggiore was driving the car last night." She looked suspiciously at Michael. "Come to think of it, how did they know to call me here at the church?"

Michael grinned at her. "Okay. I confess. They called and asked me. That's why I decided to stop by."

"We're going to see them after lunch," Victoria told him.

"So, tell us Michael," Louise said. "Is it over? Did Susanne kill Jon?"

"No one's been arrested," Michael replied.

The women recognized hedging when they heard it.

"But you think she did it?" Louise asked.

Michael shrugged. "Ma doesn't think so."

All eyes turned to Maggie. "Susanne says someone else was out there."

Michael shook his head. He didn't have to say he didn't believe her; that slow back and forth motion of his head said it all.

Chapter Twenty-eight

Maggie and Victoria decided to have lunch before heading to Tempe. They chose a small sandwich shop not far from St. Rose, where Louise joined them, enjoying a quiet hour together talking of many things—but not of murder, or potential hit-and-runs. It was an hour of peace where Maggie, Victoria and Louise could pretend they had no interest in anything more important than sewing or shopping.

Their respite was over soon enough. Maggie and Victoria drove to the campus police office and made another statement. They were shown Roman's small white car, but as they had warned on the phone, they were unable to say whether or not it was the same one that had almost run them down.

When they climbed back into her car, Maggie suggested a visit to Susanne.

"I thought you didn't know the address."

"I don't. But I think I can find it again."

And she did. They soon pulled up to the small house, where the garage door stood open. Inside were a black Toyota truck and a teal Escort with California plates. Susanne's car. Her cousin must own the truck.

Susanne didn't open the door right away. They saw a curtain at the side of the entrance move, then return to its former place. Finally she cracked the door open; a chain remained attached.

"Susanne, please. I need to talk to you," Maggie pleaded.

"What do you want?" Her voice was scratchy, as though she'd been crying. A lot.

"I hope you're not mad at me for telling the police where to find the car. You must understand that I couldn't keep it a secret forever."

There was a loud sigh, then the door closed. For a minute, Maggie worried that she wouldn't open it again. But they heard the sound of the chain being slipped, then the door reopened. This time, it swung back enough to let them enter.

Maggie wanted to hug Suzanne, she looked so frail and tired. Her eyes were puffy and bloodshot, her face red and splotchy. But that fidgety nervous energy she had displayed on Tuesday was missing.

"Are you all right?"

Susanne clutched a tissue to her mouth, but nodded that she was. She led them into a small living room, where she fell into an overstuffed brown tweed sofa. Maggie sat beside her, and Victoria seated herself on one of the two matching chairs.

"We have to be quiet," she warned. "My cousin is sleeping."

Maggie and Victoria nodded.

"We were called down here to see if we could identify the car that almost hit us last night," Maggie explained to Susanne. She kept her voice low. "It was Roman's car they wanted us to see."

Susanne bowed her head and started to cry. Obviously, she'd been doing a lot of that today.

Maggie leaned close enough to put her arm around the young woman. "You and Roman are very special friends, aren't you?"

A softness crept into Susanne's eyes. "Roman's the best friend I ever had." She gave a loud, hiccuping sigh. "We met in New York a few years ago. Two struggiing actors, trying to make it in musical theater. It's always such a struggle. This is the best job we've ever had." She paused while she wiped her eyes and blew her nose.

"When I first went to New York, I had a friend who was already there. She'd just gotten a job in *Cats*, and I was so impressed. She had this big loft she shared with a bunch of other dancers. Her dad is an important businessman back in our hometown and he'd gotten her this nice place when she moved. I think she was kind of embarrassed about having such a great place when all the rest of us were working minimum-wage jobs trying to scrape together enough money for rent and food. So she started letting other dancers share it. And she invited me to move in while I got established. Roman was one of the dancers who bunked there."

Susanne dabbed at her eyes again, then dropped the used tissues on the coffee table. "We became very close. Our relationship has been kind of rocky, but we always manage to stay friends. When we both got parts in this tour, we were so happy." She sniffed, wiping at her damp cheeks with her fingers. Maggie offered a tissue, and she blew her nose and wiped her eyes. "Then I met Jon Hunter, and everything really started going wrong. He was such a good-looking guy and he could be so charming. He had the lead of course and he did such a great job with it. I was in love."

Maggie stared at her in surprise. For an actress, Susanne seemed to be mighty short in the ego department. Jon might have had the title role but she played the female lead. Not only was the part bigger, it was so demanding that it was routinely split between two actresses so that one person would not have to do all eight weekly shows.

"So you started dating Jon?"

Suzanne shook her head. "No. But he knew I liked him and he would do things to cause trouble between Roman and me." She stared down into her lap. "He never understood that our friendship was a lot more important to us than any possible romance."

"That's because he didn't have any friendships like that himself," Victoria said.

Susanne, surprised by her statement, looked up. "Yes, I think you're right." She smiled at Victoria, her lips tilting only slightly before pulling down once more.

"Roman tried to warn me about him, but I wouldn't listen. I thought he was just jealous." She reached over to an end table for more tissues.

"You must realize that the police think you killed him because you had his car," Victoria said quietly.

Susanne nodded miserably. "They do think I did it. The questioning was horrible. I told them the story over and over again. And they just kept at it, going over and over it again and again." The tears started to run down her cheeks. "No wonder Tanya was so upset."

"Having Jon's car in your garage is pretty clear evidence," Maggie reminded her.

Susanne just shook her head, wiping ineffectively at her wet cheeks. It was all getting to be too much.

"Did Roman try to run us down last night?" Maggie asked.

Susanne pulled more tissues from the box, dabbing at the tears which continued to stream down her face. "I don't know. I didn't see him last night after the show. The police were waiting to talk to me. He did tell me he'd left a note on your car. He was worried about all the questions you were asking. He knew how nervous and scared I was, and he figured if you talked to me I'd just fall apart and tell you everything. Which I did."

"There has to be some way to determine what happened." Maggie insisted.

"I don't see how." Susanne was equally insistent. "Roman and I have gone over it over and over again. It was just the two of us out there. The person who killed Jon had to have already been there. In the desert, in the middle of nowhere. This person came and killed Jon and left without me hearing him? No one is going to believe a story like that. I can't even believe it and I was there."

Maggie and Victoria exchanged a look. She was right.

"Could someone have followed you from the restaurant?" Maggie asked. "Jeff maybe?"

Susanne shook her head. "I don't see how. And why would Jeff want to follow us anyway?" She seemed honestly puzzled.

"What about Roman?" Maggie liked this scenario even better. He could have seen them leave together and followed in a jealous rage. She repeated her thoughts to Susanne.

Susanne frowned. "Roman can get into a temper and I've seen him throw things a couple of times." She shook her head. "Still, I just don't see how he could have followed us without us knowing it. It was so dark and deserted out there."

"People have been known to drive with their headlights out," Victoria reminded her, her voice soft and gentle.

"Well, maybe it's possible," Susanne conceded. "But he's gone over this with me again and again since it happened. I don't see how he could do that if he was the one who did it. He's an okay actor but he's mostly a dancer. And that would take some real heavy-duty acting."

Maggie got up. All of a sudden, she felt tired to the bone. "Well, thank you for seeing us Susanne. I know this is a difficult time for you."

"I just hope I don't lose my job." She was dabbing at her eyes again. "This is such a great job."

Ah, the resilience of youth, Maggie thought. From agonizing over going to jail, to worrying about her job. She put her arm around Susanne and gave her shoulders a squeeze. "You'll just have to be strong."

As they drove back home, Maggie and Victoria discussed their impressions of Susanne.

"She's certainly upset," Victoria commented.

Maggie had to agree. "But I think she's relieved to be rid of that car."

"And of course she has every right to be upset at being the chief suspect."

Maggie kept her eyes on the road. "I don't know what to think anymore, Victoria. I find it hard to believe that Susanne is involved. But she did lie to us the first time—remember? She said she hadn't told a soul what happened that night. But she did tell Roman." Maggie was silent while she passed through a busy intersection. "And that story! Like she said, no one can believe it. How could someone come out of the desert in the middle of the night and hit Jon on the head with a rock? Then, disappear without her seeing or hearing a thing?" She shook her head in disbelief. "Though Roman is looking better as a suspect. Such a shame, though, that good-looking young man."

"He is a lovely dancer," Victoria said. Then she chuckled. "You know, you'd think a performer would come up with a better story."

Maggie found she could chuckle, too. In fact, it felt good to laugh about it. "You're right. If we wrote this up and submitted it as a movie plot, we'd be laughed out the door." Then she sobered. "It's the main reason I tend to believe her."

Chapter Twenty-nine

"So the case is solved. And the car did turn out to be the most important clue," Clare declared. "And to think that you were the one to find it, Maggie."

The Quilting Bee members were stretching a new quilt into their frame on Friday morning, just as they had been doing almost two weeks ago when Clare entered and told them about Jonathan's death. Pulling the backing fabric into place, they listened intently while Maggie and Louise told of their visit with Susanne.

"So have the police arrested her?" Clare wanted to know.

"No. There isn't enough evidence to arrest her. But Michael said there would be a lot of intense questioning. And there may be some evidence later, after the results of various tests come back from the lab." Maggie sighed. "It's so sad. I got to know all those young people and I liked them. I just can't believe that Susanne might be a killer."

"But nothing else makes any sense," Victoria reminded her.

"No." Maggie had to agree.

"Couldn't Jeff have followed them out there?" Clare asked, still devoted to her favorite theory. "He and Tanya left the restaurant together. They could have followed Jon and Susanne. He could have stopped his car farther back and walked up to where they were. If he didn't use his headlights and stopped the car engine the same time they did, they wouldn't have seen or heard it."

"Looking at it that way, Roman is a better suspect," Maggie answered. "He'd already told Susanne he thought Jon was toying with her. She said their relationship was rocky but that they always remained great friends. He was very protective of her. I noticed that the Tuesday after the murder, when he escorted her from the theater."

Anna spoke quietly. "That's why he tried to scare you off."

"And he'll go to jail for that, too," Edie declared firmly. "Can't go around trying to run people down."

Maggie and Victoria exchanged a significant look. Maggie sighed. Well, she'd find out eventually. "We're not pressing charges."

"What?" The word was almost a shriek.

"He didn't harm us at all," Victoria said. "We talked it over and decided not to do anything."

"Besides," Maggie reminded them, "there wasn't any evidence against him. No one could identify the car. No one could tell who was driving. So I doubt they could have prosecuted anyway."

Edie's outrage left her momentarily tongue-tied. Not that the others minded. Maggie decided to speak before she recovered. "Well, Judy got to be a good friend, and I'm grateful for that. I invited her to come out next Monday to watch us work. She's interested in learning to quilt."

Louise nodded. "Piercing would be a nice hobby for her, something she could work on while she's on the road."

"I hadn't thought of that."

"And is she seeing Michael?" Anna asked with a sweet smile.

Maggie answered with a wide grin. "He isn't saying much but I know they've gone out."

"I like Judy," Victoria said.

"So do I," Maggie added with another grin.

They finished stretching the batting out over the taunt backing and spread out the top. A Bear's Claw done in plaids, the top had a more masculine look than many of the pastel quilts they made. Louise had pieced it, after seeing a similar one on display at a local quilt shop. She thought it would give more variety to their auction.

Maggie pulled the top toward her, holding it steady while Louise pinned at the opposite side. "I still think that there's something we're all missing." Maggie didn't have to tell the others that her mind had returned to Jonathan's murder. "I keep going back to the disappearance of Ed Hunter."

"Jon's father?" Louise asked.

"Yes. It was twenty years ago, but it still bothers me. I talked to some old neighbors about it. We all agreed it was strange. And supposedly Carmen and Jon tried to find him later. They had no luck at all. He'd simply disappeared. We agreed—he was the type who might take off but he wasn't smart enough to disappear without a trace."

Louise finished pinning at her side of the frame and Maggie started on hers.

"You think he died? Or was murdered?" Clare's eyes widened. "But how would that tie in with Jon's death?"

"I wish I knew. It's just some kind of intuition, I guess." Maggie's voice was troubled. "There's something there, just out of reach. . . ."

Early the next morning, Maggie headed out to the ranch. She said a quick hello to Sara and the boys then led Chestnut out for a ride. She'd decided to revisit her memories. It was time to lay aside those haunting old dreams and go on with her life. And while she was out there, she would stop near the place where Jon's body was found and say a prayer for his soul.

Maggie enjoyed her ride. The temperature was a pleasant eighty degrees. The wildflowers were almost gone but the brittlebush was still blooming, painting the desert with its bright yellow flowers. Her leisurely ride took her over the ranch property Hal had up for sale. She wanted to take one last look at it. Except for developers, there hadn't been any firm offers but Hal said that interest from individuals was picking up.

Finally, Maggie reached the spot where Jon's body had been found. It was a beautiful bit of land but forever sullied in her mind by the events of that early morning. Dismounting, she bowed her head and said a prayer for the repose of Jon's soul. And because she needed to put her old memories to rest, she added a short prayer for herself. She was just turning to remount Chestnut when a voice startled her out of her reverie. Harley stood about ten feet away, his old horse standing beside him, his dog at his heels.

"Harley Stoner, you just about scared me into a heart attack!"

"Just saying good day, Maggie." He looked slightly chastened by her discomposure.

"That's okay. No harm done." Her mind must have been pretty far away not to have heard him ride up but she managed to pull herself back together with a minimum of effort and summon up a smile.

"I understand that you and Carmen had a good time renewing your acquaintance." Her eyes twinkled. Harley might not be her type but he was a hardworking man, a good provider. He'd looked almost handsome when he'd appeared at the funeral in his best clothes. And she was sure he would never hit a woman. Maybe there *was* something there. For Carmen's sake, she hoped so, because she liked the changes she saw in Carmen when she mentioned Harley. Carmen had called Maggie the night before to say she was returning to L.A. Her service had called about a job, if she could get back right away. But she'd talked as if she would be back soon and Maggie suspected the reason for that stood in front of her.

To her surprise Harley actually looked embarrassed at her mention of Carmen and him as a couple. "Yeah. Well, Carmen is a good woman. Good-looking, too."

"Yes. It's about time she thought of marrying again."

"Hmmm. You think she might like to?"

Maggie looked carefully at Harley. He was sincere; he really wanted to know.

Maggie nodded slowly. "I think she might be ready to think about remarrying." She smiled. "To the right man." A sudden thought occurred to her. "Did she ever divorce Ed?"

Harley gave her a sharp look. "He was declared dead after seven years. She had to get a detective to look for him."

"So that's why," Maggie murmured. That explained why she and Jon had tried to find him then. Maggie had never understood that.

"What was that?"

"Nothing. Thinking out loud."

"See, there was some insurance. Not much, but he had to be dead before she could get it. She used that for Jon's college money."

"Ahh." Maggie patted Chestnut on the neck. The old horse was a source of comfort for her as much as this land. "I was talking to some of the old neighbors. We were saying Ed must have died shortly after leaving. He wasn't smart enough to disappear so completely."

Harley was watching her intently. It made her uncomfortable, for no reason that she could explain.

"I heard the oddest thing, though. Jimmy told me he saw Ed that last night, walking into the desert around here," Maggie gestured around her. "With a bottle. Doesn't seem like he would have run off if he was on a binge."

Harley looked uncomfortable. "He did that a lot. Went off with a bottle and got roaring drunk. That's when he'd—" He stopped suddenly, his words trailing off into nothingness.

The idea Maggie had been trying so hard to grasp seemed to be coming closer. "When he'd . . . ?" she asked.

"Nothing."

"That's when he hit Carmen, isn't it? And maybe Jon, too."

Harley was backing away. He bumped against the side of his horse nibbling contentedly at some desert grass.

"You knew he beat her, didn't you?" Maggie persisted. "He was a lousy, evil man."

Suddenly Maggie knew where her mind had been leading her. "You know, I wonder if Carmen didn't kill Ed herself." Now that she said it, she couldn't believe it hadn't occurred to her earlier. "Fighting back, you know. It happens now and juries let the woman off. Maybe Jon even helped her." A new thought came to her and her unruly mouth let it out before she could catch it. "Maybe a friendly neighbor helped her dispose of the body."

Harley's eyes had almost glazed over and his hands opened and closed at his sides. "Carmen wouldn't have done that. She's too sweet and gentle."

Maggie began to feel nervous. If her theory was correct, Harley might possibly be dangerous. And that look he had in his eyes at the moment—it reminded her of a man she'd once seen being taken into the hospital in a straitjacket.

Her eyes shifted to the horse behind him. As she'd suspected, strapped to the western saddle was a holder for a shotgun. Filled. The old-timers never went out without a rifle or a shotgun.

She stared again at Harley, at the strange look in his eyes. How far was he willing to go to protect Carmen? Did he have something to do with Jon's death too? But why, given his tender feelings for Jon's mother?

Uncertain how to maneuver herself out of this possibly dangerous situation she'd gotten herself into, Maggie decided to keep talking. Besides, she was naturally curious and wanted to know what had happened. And Harley could probably tell her. "Jimmy thinks that Ed fell in the mountains somewhere and died. He said there are places there where a body would never be found."

Harley looked wary. "Ed couldn't handle his liquor."

Maggie was feeling more anxious. The thought that Harley might have helped Ed along on his last journey was impossible to dismiss. Maggie moved closer to Chestnut's side. Today she did have her cell phone handy. But it was in a holder, clipped to the side of her belt. Could she remove it and call 911 without causing Harley to panic and perhaps kill her? It was time to get back into the saddle. But she kept her eyes on Harley, waiting for her chance.

"So you hated Ed for the way he treated Carmen. She's always been a very pretty woman. You were probably walking out in the desert late, the way you do, just enjoying the night with your dog. And you saw him walking out that night, the bottle in his hand. And you knew what would happen when he finished it up and went home."

Harley was near tears. "He would have gone home and hit that beautiful little woman. He was a no-good bully and the world is better without him."

Maggie had to agree with the sentiment, but she couldn't condone his method. She swallowed hard. Words failed her. How could she ask someone if he had killed a man? But her expression must have asked it for her.

"I didn't kill him, if that's what you're thinking." Harley looked down at Boy, who had come over and sat down beside him. The dog seemed to be aware of his master's distress and had come to offer the comfort of his presence. Maggie took the moment of Harley's distraction to climb into the saddle. Maybe he was telling the truth. Maybe not. But he still had that half-crazed look in his eyes.

"I saw him walking out with that bottle, too. He got real mean when he was drunk. Real mean. I went over to his place and camped out near the house. Figured if he came back and tried to do something . . ." His voice drifted off, letting Maggie imagine what it was he might have done. "Stayed there all night and never saw him. Figured it was safe to leave after sunrise. Figured he'd passed out somewhere and was sleeping it off."

Harley reached down and scratched the dog's head. The gesture was so touching Maggie thought surely she must be wrong. Despite the warm day, she felt chills running up her back. "Did anyone look for him when he didn't come back?"

"Some of us went out and looked for him; didn't look too hard." Maggie was shocked at the dry disinterest in Harley's voice.

"He was so universally disliked. Didn't it occur to the police that someone might have killed him?"

Harley shrugged. "They interviewed people. Decided he was tired of his family and took off. Didn't do much looking for him after that."

Maggie felt safer now that she was mounted on the back of the large horse. But Harley had a horse too. She continued to stare into Harley's eyes. "You often have insomnia, don't you, Harley? I remember you telling me once how you come out here and walk late at night, just you and Boy. Look at the stars and enjoy the peace of the untouched desert." Perhaps he *had* seen what happened to Jon. He could easily have been nearby.

"I love this country," Harley said. "I wasn't born here, but as soon as I saw it, I knew I was home. I love it." His voice was soft but every word was distinct. "It's a damn shame what people are doing to the desert now." That almost insane gleam returned to his eyes. "Just bulldozing the land—building, building, and building some more. They could build nice houses without destroying what's here but they don't. They have to have everything. They take out the saguaros, uproot the mesquite trees. All they want is bigger and bigger houses. Fountains and pools. Fountains—in the desert!"

He was speaking fast now, the passion of his feelings evident. "They destroy plants that have been here for hundreds of years, reconfigure the land, divert the old washes."

The truth came to Maggie with a sudden flash and she knew she was in big trouble. She could see it clearly. Everything she'd learned about Jon led her to believe he'd want the biggest and the best. He'd brought Susanne out here, shouting his plans to her as she lingered by the car. Grandiose plans.

Maggie was at "the scene of the crime" with someone she suddenly knew had done the deed. Her hands tightened on the reins, ready to flee at the first opportunity.

Harley's eyes had that glazed look once again. "You know"—his voice was soft, low, resigned—"you always were too smart for your own good."

Maggie knew she should leave now. It would be simple for her to press her heels into Chestnut's sides and race across the desert. He had a horse too, but she'd have a head start. Still she hesitated, her eyes locked on Harley's.

To Maggie's amazement, a tear squeezed out of Harley's right eye and trailed slowly down his cheek. "It was a craziness came over me." He seemed to be retreating into another world. "I was out here just walking. And I hear this voice, floating out across the desert. Loud, raucous. Some fool of a man was standing there, shouting about all the harm he was going to cause to this beautiful land." Tears were streaming from both eyes now but Harley made no move to wipe them away. Boy whimpered. "He was going to destroy this wonderful place, to add another enormous house and a lot of fancy toys. Swimming pools and tennis courts and heaven knows what else. I couldn't help myself. I couldn't take it any more. I actually saw red—just a haze before my eyes. And then the next moment I was standing there with a rock in my hands and a body at my feet."

Maggie kept her eyes on him. Obviously, the man was unstable. But how sick was he? She kept watching him, kept him talking. But she was ready to take off on Chestnut the moment he got too close.

"It was an abomination. This beautiful, pristine land. It's where I come to find peace, to find my soul. And he was going to destroy it."

Maggie listened, amazed. She hadn't known Harley could speak so eloquently.

"The next day. . . . I learned who it was the next day." His voice choked on a sob. "I died a little inside."

"Does Carmen know?" But Maggie realized the answer had to be no. Carmen could never have dated her son's killer.

"Of course not. It's been a nightmare. I love that woman. Always have."

"So you come out here trying to find solace."

Harley nodded. But his eyes were bleak. Chances were he wouldn't encounter much peace here any more. Maggie found it in her heart to say a silent prayer for him.

His sentences became fragmented, his eyes frantic.

"Can't sleep. Walk till I'm exhausted. . . ."

He took a step toward Maggie, reaching out for her.

Maggie didn't wait to see what he was going to do. Her nervous control shattered and she dug her heels into Chestnut's sides, taking off into the desert. She wouldn't worry about calling now—she had to get away first, then she could pause long enough to dial 911. She risked a quick look back, long enough to see that Harley had mounted and seemed to be coming after her. Her breath caught in her throat and she tried to urge Chestnut to greater speed. She was a good horse, but she was no two-year-old. Thankfully, Harley's mount wasn't either.

She hoped she'd put some distance between them when a shot rang out, startling Chestnut into a burst of speed. Maggie's breath rasped in and out of her parted lips. In the desert foothills, it was impossible to tell how far away the shooter was.

Maggie pushed Chestnut as hard as she dared, not looking back. It would take too much time and she needed every bit of concentration. She unhooked the cell phone from her belt, managed to dial the three magic numbers. She wondered if her message sounded as scrambled and insane to the operator as it did to her. Yet every word was true.

By the time she reached the ranch house, the initial shock of discovery was gone and she was more saddened than scared. But she trotted Chestnut around to the front of the house, hoping the police were already there.

Epilogue

The Brownes were gathered for Sunday brunch and they had appeared in force. All the brothers were there with their wives. The grandchildren were there. Even the Quilting Bee members were in attendance.

It had been over a month since Maggie had learned the truth of Jonathan's death, and faced down Harley Stoner. The *Phantom of the Opera* tour had moved on. Hal was going to close on the piece of property that had precipitated the death of Jonathan Hunter. A young family had bought it; they planned to build a mid-sized house and keep a few horses for the children.

"I'm so glad it's all over, even though it ended badly," Maggie said, when the subject of Jonathan, inevitably, came up.

"Well, it depends on what you call 'badly,' " Frank replied.

"Saved the taxpayers a lot of money shooting himself that way," Edie declared.

"I understand what Ma means," Hal said. "We grew up around Harley and it's a shame any of this happened."

"I've thought over those last minutes in the desert," Maggie said, "and I don't think he was coming after me to kill me. He was crying, really upset about the fact that he'd killed his sweetheart's only son. I think he was just following me, maybe trying to explain he didn't mean to do it. But I was so upset thinking I was right there next to a killer, a killer with a rifle, I panicked."

Soothing noises came from all sides, voices assuring her she had every right to panic.

"I can't help thinking that he went a little crazy after you found him out," Hal said. "I can just see him taking that shotgun from his saddle and walking out into the desert. Right there to the same spot where he killed Jon, too."

Michael had been listening to his brother and now he added his opinion. "When the DNA evidence they collected off the murder weapon came back, they were able to match it with Harley. He'd scraped his hands when he handled the rock and the lab was able to get DNA off the bits of skin that they found. So he may have been arrested for Jon's murder eventually. But it wasn't a lot of evidence, so there's no telling what would have happened at a trial. It could have gone on for a long time. I can't help thinking that he did it for Carmen."

The others all exclaimed over this reasoning, asking him to explain.

"How could killing himself have been for Carmen?" Merrie asked.

"He knew it would have been painful for her. Not only the shame she would feel that a man she cared for killed her son but going through a long court proceeding. I think he decided to just do it and get it over with. That way Carmen has a chance to begin to heal."

"That's a nice way to look at it." Maggie stared at her youngest son in surprise. What a romantic he was. Was he being influenced by his continued communication with Judy? He'd taken off a few days to drive her to St. Louis for the next leg of the tour.

"It's a nice sentiment," Hal said, "but my thinking is that he just didn't want to face up to what he'd done. Strange as he was, Harley was a proud man. A lawyer would have wanted him to plead insanity, of course. What he told you about that night, Ma, makes it sound like that's just what it was, too. But I can't help thinking he preferred to die rather than be ridiculed as a crazy old man."

"I'll take the ending of a mystery novel any day," Clare decided. "In my books, the bad guys always get punished."

"Well, he was punished," Louise observed. "Though perhaps more in his own mind by the guilt he felt. Killing the only son of the woman he loved . . ."

"I can't believe Carmen came back for his funeral." Anna shook her head.

Maggie had found that hard to fathom, too. But she'd finally worked it out. "I think it gave the whole episode closure for her. Hearing what happened in the desert that day explained a lot. She discovered that Ed hadn't run out on her after all. And she was able to mourn for both Jon and Harley and start to put that aside."

"And her coming gave us a chance to give her the memory quilt," Victoria reminded them.

When Maggie heard that Carmen was coming for the funeral, she'd invited her to attend the Quilting Bee, where the presentation had been made. Carmen had been touched to tears by the beautiful quilt, with its signatures of all her son's co-workers and its decorative red roses.

"She cried all over it," Edie said gruffy.

Much to Edie's surprise, everyone laughed.

"That sounds like a fitting tribute to me." Sara's voice was thick with laughter. "Heavens, I cried when Ma gave us our wedding quilt. I expect a quilt made in memory of a deceased son would be even more emotional to look at."

"Well, I guess," Edie admitted grudgingly, to more laughter.

Maggie stood to replenish the coffeepot. As she made her way inside she looked over the tables on the patio. All her family and friends were here. She was a lucky woman. Carmen had lost a lot when she thought her husband deserted her: her dignity, her confidence, her pride. She'd sought to prevent losing the other person she loved, her son Jon, by almost smothering him with love. And now she was alone.

As Maggie returned across the patio with the refilled pot, she let her eyes rest momentarily on each of her four sons. She might have wonderful memories of five little boys, but they no longer haunted her. Her four boys had grown into wonderful men—hardworking, caring, contributing members of society. After her dreams and detecting and turmoil, Maggie now realized how important it was to live in the present. She planned to enjoy her family and friends every day.

As Maggie took her seat, someone clicked a spoon against a glass. She looked around just as Hal stood, his face split by a wide grin, his orange juice glass raised high. "A toast—for our very own Miss Marple. To Ma!"

Addendum

Make your own signature quilt like the one the Quilting Bee presented to Carmen. To make one block, cut three strips of fabric, two inches by five inches; this includes a quarter-inch seam allowance. One strip, the one for the signature, should be cut from white or off-white fabric. The other two should be in a print and color of your choice. Sew the two colored strips to either side (the five-inch side) of the white strip using a quarter inch seam allowance. This makes a four-and-a-half-inch finished block. Cut a piece of freezer paper approximately five inches square, and place it *shiny side down* on the *wrong* side of your block. Press with a hot iron until the paper sticks to the fabric. Now it's ready to be autographed. Use permanent ink fabric pens for the signatures. After the block has been signed, remove the freezer paper. Arrange the blocks in a pleasing manner and sew together using a one-quarter-inch seam.